For more than forty years,
Yearling has been the leading name
in classic and award-winning literature
for young readers.

Yearling books feature children's
favorite authors and characters,
providing dynamic stories of adventure,
humor, history, mystery, and fantasy.

Trust Yearling paperbacks to entertain,
inspire, and promote the love of reading
in all children.

OTHER YEARLING BOOKS
YOU WILL ENJOY

Sweet Thang

allison whittenberg

A YEARLING BOOK

Visit us on the Web! www.randomhouse.com/kids

Educators and librarians, for a variety of teaching tools, visit us at
www.randomhouse.com/teachers

ISBN: 978-0-440-42086-6

Reprinted by arrangement with Delacorte Press

Printed in the United States of America

June 2007

10 9 8 7 6 5 4 3 2

First Yearling Edition

This book is dedicated to the memory of

Faye Marlene Whittenberg, my mother.

Acknowledgments

I'm happy that this book fell into the nurturing hands of Stephanie Lane, a super editor who found the "story" within the story.

I owe a debt of gratitude to my English and Latin teacher, Mrs. Jean Heslar, who turned me on to the power of words.

Thank you, Auntie Harriet. You were everything an auntie could be: fun, kind, and more than a little eccentric.

One

I can travel through time. Sometimes it's voluntary; sometimes it's not. Like one night, I saw a movie with these white people with dark hair—I think they were Italian. In this film, there was a funeral scene where the main character jumped the six feet into the ground after the coffin was lowered, and all of a sudden I was right back at that day. My version had black people all dressed in black and only a smattering of white people, from the nursing program she had been in. She left behind a son. She had named him Tracy John Upshaw.

She was Karyn. I knew her as Auntie; she was Daddy's little sis.

Everything annoyed me that day. I was watching Auntie Karyn in her coffin, and I knew that Auntie Karyn was watching me. At the grave site, the Reverend Whitaker led us away, saying, "There's nothing we can do now."

I didn't want to be ushered to the side, and I hated those words: *There's nothing we can do now*. Especially the word *nothing*. There had to be *something*—something that would bring her back.

Reverend Whitaker used his arm to brace, then move me. My legs felt like they might fold under me. By the limo, my relatives were sobbing in one big huddled mass.

My last look at Auntie made my chest hurt. I was only eleven, but I felt like I was having a heart attack. Auntie had always been fair, but her face was now whiter, glittering, almost like wax. All her hopes, every dream, every prayer were lost, gone. Her large penny-colored eyes were closed forever.

What was I going to do? With the rest of my life, I mean. Without her, suddenly there was all this space. Space that would have been taken up by our adventures. Taking trips around the city or going to the movies or just hanging out. I know that sounds selfish, to think of things like that. But she was so much fun, so interesting, so up-to-the-minute with her clogs and scarves and bangles and jeans with the patches on them and Jeff caps over her natural hair. I wanted to be just like her, but my mom would never let me dress like that.

Back at the house, my family gathered. Otis Redding played on the stereo, singing "Fa-Fa-Fa-Fa-Fa (Sad Song)." There was a lot of chicken. Fried, braised, broiled, roasted in a pan, stuck in a potpie. So much food. Nine trays of potato salad. Seven trays of bread pudding (Auntie Karyn's favorite dessert). Distant relatives ate heartily, even sloppily, macaroni salad sliding off their spoons onto their chins.

Only three at the time, Tracy John was asleep during most of that day. He was passed from arm to arm. Everyone wanted to hold the precious one; he was like a hot potato in reverse. Family and friends didn't leave till it was dark. Then it really sank in: *I'll never see her again.*

"I just want to know why," I sobbed into my open hands.

Daddy offered no explanation. He just came over and held me while I pulled myself together. Though he didn't sob that day, either in public or alone with me, I could see that he wasn't whole. Like the rest of us who loved her, he had a hole in the heart that would never go away.

With the sun down, my head felt lighter. My heart was heavier.

Around midnight, Uncle O called to tell us that his car had broken down by the airport. He said the engine had died. Daddy took jumper cables and my older brother, Horace, to Island Avenue to rescue him.

That night my eyes felt propped open by some unknown force. I wished Daddy had taken me with him instead of Horace. Maybe working a jack or holding a flashlight could have gotten my mind off the pain in my heart.

Nobody knew who would take Tracy John for good. Gammy had him for the rest of the week, and I thought she was going to keep him. The following week, he was with us; midweek, Gammy took him back. Then, that

Friday, I was over Uncle O's apartment, and Tracy John was there.

By the end of the month, he was back at our house, and I guessed that Tracy John was going to stay with us forever. Back then, I didn't think that would be a problem. He was small and playful, and he fit right in with Daddy; Ma; my two brothers, Horace and Leo; and me.

But within a week of Tracy John's moving into our home for good, I lost my room.

When Ma told me, I was shocked. "What!"

Daddy backed her up, repeating what she had just said.

"No, no," I pleaded. "Let him move in with Leo."

"Leo is moving in with you, Charmaine," Ma said.

"But he's a *boy*. I can't live with a boy."

"Boy, girl, don't make no matter." Daddy waved me away. "We're all family."

I turned to Ma. "I don't have any friends who share a room with their brothers."

"Then you don't have any friends who share a room with their brothers," Daddy said. "That don't mean nothing. You and your brother will live together. That's how they do it in the country."

"What country?" I asked.

Daddy shot me a look that told me it was in my best interest to be quiet. I didn't argue with Daddy. Even at the age of eleven, I was pro-life—my *own*.

Inside, though, I was mad. How could they do a thing like that to me? How did Tracy John get his own room?

Tracy John could stay with Leo, or Horace for that matter. Tracy John wouldn't even know the difference.

As worried as I had been three years before, now things had reached crisis proportions. Each day I was reminded that it was all about His Highness: the precious one, Tracy John Upshaw.

Like one day, Tracy John almost cost Daddy sixty dollars for a pair of glasses he didn't need. Ma took him to get his eyes examined for the start of the school year. Tracy John had been reading ever since he was three and a half, so he knew his letters very well. The doctor thought Tracy John should wear a strong prescription because he'd read all but the top two lines wrong. Ma took him to the eyeglass shop. Over the next two hours, Tracy John tried on children's frames. He didn't like a single pair.

When they came home, Tracy John pointed at me and said, "I want glasses like her."

Her? Her! I only lived in the same house as he did. He'd known me his whole life. I wasn't a "her" to be pointed at like some stranger on the street. I was his blood relative: Charmaine. He could have called me that, or Maine, like everyone else did.

"You tried on glasses like that, honey," Ma said to him, all patience and understanding.

"I want *her* glasses," Tracy John repeated fiercely, as if he was going to grab them right from my face.

The next day, Ma, pixie-faced Tracy John, and I went all the way to downtown Philly to another eyeglass store. This time Tracy John spent two hours trying on forty-seven pairs of frames. I was about to blow my stack. Ma alternated between "Do you like this one, sugar?" and "How about this, pumpkin?" Even the salesclerk was in on the act, calling him peanut. They patted him on the head after lovingly fitting each frame around his ears. It was outrageous.

The other patrons smiled and cooed at him, and over time they formed a small circle around him. In the end, Tracy John settled on a pair of glasses that looked nothing like my octagonal frames. He chose small black wire glasses that looked a little Ben Franklinish.

The shop promised to put in a rush job on account of the doctor's saying Tracy John was half blind. Ma paid a ten-dollar deposit, leaving a balance of more than fifty dollars. We got on the number 13 trolley back to our home in Dardon. No sooner were we on the streetcar than Tracy John had a change of heart. He suddenly tugged at Ma's arm and said, "I don't want glasses. I see twenty."

Ma gave him a quizzical look.

He was insistent. "I see twenty."

We got off at the next stop and caught the other trolley going back to Center City. At the eye doctor, it was concluded. In fact, Tracy John did see twenty. Twenty-twenty.

So what had Tracy John done the previous day? Just made up letters like some fool. When Ma told Daddy, he just chuckled at it like it was funny.

Later that evening, Daddy was in the living room, Tracy John cuddled in his lap sneaking sips of his beer. That kid was too much. A few times a night, Daddy

6

encouraged him. Habitually, Daddy would tell him to run into the kitchen and say a bad word to Ma. Tracy John would run into the kitchen and say, "Unc told me to say 'bullshit.' " And Daddy would laugh at Ma's fit. This left me to wonder: would Tracy John have gotten away with all this mayhem if he hadn't been walking around with Auntie Karyn's face?

As I watched *The Godfather* and struggled to come back from Auntie's funeral, the phone rang. Ma answered it and told me it was for me.

I walked to the phone, wishing I had my own phone in my own room. I wanted a king-sized bed with a heavy velvet canopy where I could talk the day away. Instead I had to stretch the phone into the bathroom, close the door, and sit on the toilet lid.

I was on the phone only ten minutes. I was talking to my best friend, Millicent, about the gorgeous new boy at school, Demetrius McGee.

"Did you see him in that blue sweater, Millicent? He has to be the best-looking guy ever. He looks like a Greek god. An African Greek god," I said.

"Oh, Demetrius!" Leo and Tracy John mocked in unison behind the door.

I was endlessly heckled. They just didn't understand when I was talking about something important.

"Excuse me, Millicent," I said into the phone, and then put it to the side. I opened the bathroom door.

"Will you two get out of here!"

They laughed all over themselves, especially Tracy John, with his sickeningly sweet, squinched-up face.

"Shoo, y'all," I said, chasing them back into the living room.

As soon as I was back to the phone, my mother told me to get off.

"Millicent, I gotta go." I hung up.

I had to have my own room! I could play my own eight-tracks—my Roberta Flacks and Al Greens. I craved privacy. Our house was worse than Watergate: filled with bugs, and not the kind that you could spray with Raid. Half the time, I couldn't even get the bathroom to myself when I was talking on the phone. There was no place to get away from everyone. I'd go in one room, and Leo and Tracy John would be in there. In another, Horace would have a girl or his recruiter over. He was about to go to basic training. I'd go downstairs, and Daddy and his pinochle friends would be there. Ma would be in the kitchen, running the faucet, clattering the pots and pans or silverware, and I would try to slip away before she had a chance to see me and ask me to help her stir butter into the beans or mix the gravy or mashed potatoes.

Dejected, I went to my half of "my" room. This had to be worse than a jail cell. At least Leo kept his side of the room neat. He always picked up after himself and had the footlocker organized well.

I thought of *The Godfather* and turned the lights off, then drew the curtains, shutting out the streetlight. I was cold. It was going to be a hard winter. Soon I'd have to sleep with my socks on.

I couldn't sleep, so I thought about her.

Usually, it worked the other way: I'd wake in the night

thinking of her. I'd lift my head from the pillow so that I could hear. I'd wait, in the nothingness of three in the morning—or maybe four. Remembering the quick shuffle. The hiss of the waterpot. She'd be downstairs with her nurse books.

Auntie Karyn. She'd had so many interests; I was surprised she had settled on being a nurse. She used to talk about the environment, stray animals, civil rights, and the women's movement. She used to go to all these meetings and bring back buttons for me. One really funny one was *A Woman Without a Man Is Like a Fish Without a Bicycle*. I still didn't know what that meant.

It was an odd thing; just when I thought it was under control, it would hit me. Maybe it wasn't about the movie. Maybe it was that Horace was due to ship out in about a week. Horace had signed up for the service after graduating from Dardon Senior High in June and a long summer of Daddy's badgering him: "No son of mine is living in this house and not working." At least the Vietnam War was over, but our family would still be broken up.

Time.

Occasional letters still came, and occasional phone calls, from people who I supposed had been on Mars and had had no idea she'd been killed. They'd want to know details—as if to recall the details wasn't painful for us. Daddy would handle it by providing curt commentary:

"She died."

"She was twenty-four."

"Yeah."

"Then he shot himself."

9

"Yeah, he should've done that first."

"Yeah, it's that kind of world."

People always said the same thing when they learned of her passing. They said she was so nice/she was so pretty/it was such a shame.

Three years after her death, I was still trying to make sense of it. And, to be honest, I don't think I ever will.

Two

What is black? Is it all about lotion or hair-care products? Without those two topics, the girls at my school would have had nothing to talk about. Millicent, Cissy, and I were the only exceptions.

My own nap curls didn't take well to being tampered with. Each Sunday morning, Ma stunned them into semistraightness with a hot comb. That was all they'd put up with.

Millicent was tall and thin like me and never straightened her shoulder-length hair. She had to do her hair herself, and she didn't do much. She just wore it in a fuzzy french braid.

Cissy was short and overweight, and her hair was overpermed and broken off.

We were the only girls left in the ninth grade whose hair was not straightened within a centimeter of its life.

And we didn't care if there was a little ash on our legs or elbows.

Though Dardon Junior High was overwhelmingly black, there was still segregation. There were the long-haired girls' table, the jock table, the nerd table. . . . The noise in the lunchroom pounded against my eardrums. I let out a labored sigh as I stared at the queen of the long-haired girls' table, Dinah Coverdale. Dinah's hair hung loose and shiny in deep silkened waves of amber. Her gray eyes looked almost spooky. She had already developed a womanly figure, filling out her sweater and slacks, and she walked around like she owned the world. The sad part about it was she did.

My intense dislike for her went back to the fourth grade, when it had come down to the two of us in a class spelling bee. The final word was *solidarity*, and she mixed the *d* with the *t*. It flipped to me, and effortlessly, I spelled it right. Later on in the schoolyard, she called me Buckwheat.

I didn't have a comeback. I just absorbed it.

I thought divine justice would step in and make all her silken locks fall out while my hair turned free flowing.

Ha.

I mused, over my half peanut-butter-and-jelly sandwich, upon how Dinah still had hair like a model from a perm box, beautiful and bouncy. Her breasts too were beautiful and bouncy. I wondered whether I would grow breasts like that if I ate more.

"Are there more light-skinned blacks or dark-skinned blacks?" I asked.

"Dark. Look at Africa," Cissy said, munching on the second of her sandwiches. Her problem was the opposite of mine. Cissy's breasts, beneath her blouse, were spilling beyond the borders of her bra.

"I'm talking about Africans in America," I said.

"Not all Africans are dark," Millicent said. "Especially not the white ones."

"There's no such thing as a white African," Cissy said.

They had both forgotten my question.

"We outnumber them, so why do we let them rule everything?" I asked.

"That's the way white works. There aren't many of them either," Cissy said.

"In America?" Millicent asked.

"No, I'm talking about the world," I said.

"Yeah, but there ain't any whites in Africa," Cissy said.

They'd *completely* forgotten my question.

"Black is beautiful, right?" I asked.

There was a long pause before they said what they thought they should say: "Well, yeah."

• • •

With Lysol and bright yellow gloves, I was stuck cleaning the bathroom. That was just one of my after-school chores. I found a toenail. It looked male. Yuck. I spied on my brothers and cousin out the window. Raking leaves, taking out the garbage, mowing the lawn, shoveling snow, and helping Daddy clean the gutter along the roof—those were their jobs. That kept them busy year-round, theoretically. Yet, as opposed to actually *working*, like me, the boys did more playing than raking the maple leaves. Horace and Leo tossed Tracy John around. They moved him from pile to pile, and buttery yellow pieces took off in flight.

Every now and then, Daddy went out there and observed their nonprogress. He'd tell them not to work "tit to tit." Spread out, they'd get more accomplished.

They still threw lion-colored leaves, roaring, as soon as Daddy's back was turned.

My dad usually came home from his twelve-hour day around five-thirty in the evening. He was five foot ten. I wasn't taller than him, but I was gaining. He was medium brown in complexion and sported a trim mustache. He wore his hair in a short Afro with licks off to the left and right where it was falling out. He had a wonderful wide smile, a broad nose, and a big voice that always made it seem like he had something important to say, even when he didn't. He grew up in West Philly, and besides Auntie Karyn, he had two brothers: Uncle E, who'd been in and out of jail over a glossary of minor offenses, and Uncle O, who had over the summer moved back to Wilmington after a failed marriage. Daddy was Pisces, the fish.

At five foot seven, I was already taller than my five-foot-two ma, but most people said I looked exactly like her because we had the same mahogany complexion. A Gemini, she had warm eyes, a soft smile, and something I really envied: long hair—long enough to put into a pony-tail. It was a good grade of hair too. Ma had the gentlest form of prettiness. She didn't wear makeup or nail polish. She always wore simple dresses. Her hobbies were even more basic than Daddy's were. She liked to sew and cook and go to church. She was originally from down South and spoke with an accent. She came from one of those ridiculously large families and was one of fourteen. She was the only person in her family to have ventured above the Mason-Dixon Line.

Though their eldest son was about to join the army, Daddy and Ma were in only their mid- and early thirties. They had been married very early in life. Very, very early—yet not too early for my brother to have been conceived. There's a copy of their marriage license in the drawer with the family Bible that dates their marriage ten months prior to Horace's birth. Yet there is an alternate license that's kept in the back of the closest under Ma's coin collection. After finding that one, I did a counting-back exercise, only to discover that Horace had been born after a miraculous three months of gestation. I asked Ma why they had two marriage licenses. She told me to stop looking through her things. Conclusion: my parents were determined to appear respectable, even if they had to lie to do so.

Ma called the boys in for supper. As we Upshaws sat around the family table in a moment of silence, my father had both hands up to the Lord. Horace, Leo, and Ma had their eyes closed, but Tracy John had his eyes wide open and his legs kicking under the table. I glared at him. Tracy John one-upped me by sticking out his tongue.

As Ma served the meat loaf, Tracy John didn't speak.

He just pointed. He kept pointing at things until someone noticed and passed him what he wanted. I hated when he did that. What, was he too precious to speak?

Tracy John was also selective in his eating habits. He ate the food he liked and ate around the food he didn't like.

"Tracy's not eating his beets," I told the table.

"Now, don't just eat the meat. Finish the vegetables on your plate," Daddy told him.

"They don't taste good," Tracy John said.

"You're a man; you can take it," Daddy assured him.

"Be a man! Be a man!" Horace howled, cheering him on like a coach.

Tracy John chewed, making a prune face. "Maine always tells," he said, but he continued eating the beets, making his face more torn up with each bite. He squinted. His nose crinkled. No one else on Earth could put such emotion into eating. Begrudgingly, I could admit what everyone else knew. He was a cute kid. He had really dewy skin, and his lips always looked wet.

As Ma went to the kitchen for more rolls, the subject switched from beets to the army.

"Seven days left of freedom," Leo said to Horace.

"Six days and a wake-up," Horace corrected.

"You got the lingo down at least," Daddy said.

Ma came back with a steaming basket dressed in cloth.

At this, Tracy John perked up. He reached into the basket like everyone else.

16

"You sure we don't have to go shopping for anything, Horace?" Ma asked.

"For the last time, missy, there's no need. They take care of everything for him right down to his drawers," Daddy told her.

"I never heard of going away for that long and not taking nothing," Ma said.

"They will take you with just the clothes on your back." Daddy pointed at Horace with his fork. "Make sure they don't learn your name. And don't volunteer for nothing."

"Is that what you did, Daddy?" Leo asked.

"Leo, they knew my name the first day," Daddy said.

"Is Horace going to Korea like you did?" Leo asked.

"I asked for Hawaii," Horace said.

"You and everybody else," Daddy said.

"I just hope I don't get down South. I want to go where something's happening," Horace said.

"What's wrong with down South? You might meet the love of your life, like I did," Daddy said.

"I want to see the world," Horace said.

"Are these drills black or white?" Leo asked.

"More of us are getting into those positions," Daddy told us.

"I hope you don't encounter any racism," Ma said.

"Is there a lot of racism in the army, Daddy?" Leo asked.

"There's racism in the world," Daddy answered.

Tracy John asked, "What's racism?"

A horn blasted outside. Horace wiped his mouth and stood up. "That's Claude and them."

Daddy gestured with his knife. "Look at him all independent. You better ask somebody before you get up from this table."

"Sorry." Horace clasped his hands in prayer. "Oh, Mother, Father, may I please go out tonight?"

"You better be home at a decent time," Ma said.

Horace nodded, gave Ma a quick peck on the cheek, waved at the rest of us, and was out the door.

Claude and Horace joined under the Stripes for Buddies Program. They were both skipped to PV2 for joining together. Claude Terrell's family had a hot dog shop, Terrell's Franks, in North Philadelphia. He always said he didn't want to work there all his life, so he traded hot dogs for helmets. He and my brother had these serious 'fros. Huge and round like Tito's or Jermaine's or Michael's. They also had those sideburns that were so in right then. It was a shame what Uncle Sam was about to do to them. They'd be sheared like lambs. At any rate, over the past few weeks, Claude had done a lot of this, going out at night. Horace said that this was his last chance to whoop it up.

Ma shook her head. "That boy swears he's grown."

"He is, Miss Sweet Thang," Daddy told Ma. "He is."

She smiled, then quickly frowned. "I'm so worried about him joining that army, I don't know what to do."

"There is nothing to worry about," Daddy said. "It's just the army. Grenades are fun."

"Lord, they got my boy messing with explosives." She fanned herself from the excitement.

"And during that night-fire exercise, I'm sure he'll stay low." Daddy continued to tease Ma.

She got up from the table, taking her half-cleaned plate.

"We just got out of that Vietnam conflict. Things'll be quiet for a while," Daddy said.

"What's night fire?" Leo asked.

"It's when the troops go out after dusk and low-crawl through this mess of mud under barbed wire—they crawl and crawl and all the while bullets are flying just inches above their heads."

I heard a plate break in the kitchen.

"Women are very emotional," Daddy told us, and he motioned to me to go in and see how Ma was doing.

Though I wanted to hear more about night fire, I got up. Once I was in the kitchen, Ma promptly put me to work. She pointed to the sink and told me to wash and dry the used pots and pans. Now, washing made sense; I was all for basic cleanliness. It was the drying that I had a problem with. Didn't the air do that?

Ma was going a mile a second, sweeping the kitchen with bullet speed. After she was done, she fetched Tracy John and told him to get ready for his bubble bath.

● ● ●

I ran into the bathroom to brush my teeth and nearly fell on my butt. There was soapy water all over the floor; I didn't think that even Noah would have been safe with all that water. Tracy John was sitting in the tub, clapping his hands on the water, making waves.

19

"Stop all that splashing," I told him.

"I like splashing," he said. He continued to pat down the suds with great glee.

I growled and closed the door, figuring Ma would say something about his conduct. I hung around the area. But Ma didn't scold him at all. In fact, when she came back into the room, I saw her with a mop. A little later, she was in Tracy John's room immersed. Calm. She read him a story that had something to do with a rabbit; then she hugged him and kissed him and wished him sweet dreams, and just when I thought he would keel over from an overdose of attention, Ma had the nerve to sing to him. "Lullaby and good night . . ."

Leo walked past me.

"Ma doesn't tuck *me* in," I told him.

"Not anymore. You're a teenager," Leo said.

I listened to Ma sing some more in her southern-fried contralto.

"I want my room back," I said.

"Don't tell me you're on that again, Maine."

"I don't like him. He's rude. He makes a mess everywhere he goes. And his head is shaped funny."

"That's the same way Auntie Karyn's head was shaped," he told me, his teeth gleaming in the nearby night-light.

Hatred bubbled in my stomach, resentment settled in my throat, and I said, "He doesn't look anything like Auntie Karyn."

"No, he's just her son." Leo rolled his eyes. "You really say some dumb things."

"I'm not dumb. I was in the enrichment program," I said hastily. I'd spent elementary school in the pull-out program for the gifted.

"Whatever."

"Leo, he bothers me."

"I like him," Leo said flatly.

"What do you like about him?"

"I don't know why I like him. It doesn't matter. We're related. He's like our brother."

"He is not my brother," I said.

"Maine, we are all brothers and sisters," he insisted.

Just then, Ma emerged.

"What are y'all doing wasting time sitting outside of the door?" Ma asked. "Your homework better be finished."

"Mine is, but Leo's isn't," I told her.

"I want to see," she said.

We both ran to our room and got our assignments. Ma gave our notebooks a good up and down. "Your handwriting is neater than this. Look at all this scratched out. Copy it over," Ma told me.

"It's just a journal entry. It doesn't even count toward my grade."

"That don't make no never mind. Always do your best." She said to Leo, "This looks fine so far."

Then she turned back to me. "I want to see this by nine o'clock."

I frowned and said, "Yes, ma'am."

"And sharpen that pencil," Ma told me, then walked down the hall.

I turned to Leo as if to say *Well, doesn't this prove that the world is against me?* I snatched his paperwork up and looked it over. It did look fine. I rolled my eyes and handed it back to him.

"You know, a black man invented the pencil sharpener," Leo said, and smiled like the god of victory.

•••

I was in a good shameless snuggle of sleep due to these three things: the soft patter of the rain outside, my soft flannel sheets, and my delicious thoughts of Demetrius McGee.

"I'm not gonna let you go buck wild in your last days in this house!" Daddy hollered from downstairs.

Both Leo and I sat up in bed.

"Don't go thinking I'm gonna bail you out neither. I have already danced that tune with your uncle; it's time for a whole new number."

"Oh, he's talking about Uncle E," Leo said.

Downstairs, Daddy shouted, "Horace, I am completely ashamed of you!"

"But I didn't—" Horace began.

"Did I ask you to speak? Car thief, did I ask you to speak?" Daddy sounded like he was about to throw a natural fit.

Horace stole a car?

This was getting good. I put on my glasses, and Leo and I ran to the top of the stairs to get a better listen.

"He's sure mad," Leo said to me.

I nodded.

"Come tomorrow morning, I'll have a whole mess of things I want you to do around this house. I'm gonna have you working from can't see to can't see. You're gonna wish they'd kept you in jail."

"Oooooooh, he's grounded, and he has to do chores," someone said behind us.

Leo and I looked over our shoulders. It was Tracy John in his powder blue jammies.

"What are you doing out of bed?" I asked.

He flipped it on me. "Same thing you are."

Leo smirked at his answer.

I rolled my eyes. I was about to say something to Tracy John when I noticed that the fighting downstairs had stopped, and I heard footsteps coming upstairs.

We all scattered like crows after a scare. I was halfway down the hall before I realized I was going the wrong way. I turned, only to see Ma and Daddy flanking Horace like wardens. Ironic that I, the one with the longest legs, got caught. I quickly made something up.

"I was just getting a sip of jail," I told them. "I mean, water."

Horace grinned at my flub.

Ma told me to go back to bed.

Three

I thought that junior high would be to a student as a cat was to a mouse. It caught me off guard and tossed me around a bit, and I was convinced that after it was satisfied, it just might eat me whole. I was sure this would surprise most people since I had always gotten excellent grades and teachers held me in high regard. Yet my expectations as I advanced in school were never met. I hoped for new material, harder problems, and deeper literature—stories I'd never heard of, or at least heavier books. But it was October. I couldn't feel it. There was no ninth-grade challenge. It was like grade 8.5. This was my last stop before the real deal—high school. But it just didn't feel right.

First up, Miss Baineau taught French with lots of English subtitles. She was from Paris, and she had been just a child during World War II. She often regaled us with tales from her girlhood—how she and her three siblings had hidden in the basement during the air raids and how much she'd loved Americans. That was very interesting but had nothing to do with conjugating verbs or mastering the subjunctive mood. Since she rarely spoke in French, we learned nothing about French pronunciation or vocabulary.

Second period, my English teacher, Mr. Mand, wore these blue monochromatic patterned ties that coordinated with his shirts. He was balding on top. He was into assigning journal entries, which he never checked or collected. Currently, we were reading the poetry of Walt Whitman, aloud, page by page. Line by line. Word by word. Though I always read with spirit when it was my turn, my fellow students put nothing into the delivery.

Third period Mondays, Wednesdays, and Thursdays was music with Mr. Huckleberry, a brother who didn't put much into his class besides Every Girl Bakes Disgusting Fudge—E, G, B, D, F on the treble. Millicent and Cissy were in that class with me. Tuesdays and Fridays, I had phys ed with Miss Crathers, a heavyset woman with downy hair on the sides of her face like sideburns. So far, all we'd done was stretch for ten minutes and play field hockey for twenty minutes. If you had worked up a sweat or hit puberty, there was time for a shower. Neither one was the case with me.

Next was twenty-two-minute lunch, and that was when I really got to gab with Millicent and Cissy. No complaints there. We gossiped about horoscopes, TV shows, what was hot on the R & B charts, and my fixation, Demetrius.

After lunch, I had Mr. Gowdy for U.S. history. He loved to talk about civil rights. He was from New York and had that Brooklynese way of speaking; next to his briefcase lay a Yankees cap. I found him the most informative of all my instructors, and Millicent was in that class. Even more interesting than that, so was Demetrius.

Algebra II was fifth period. I didn't like imaginary numbers, but our teacher, Mrs. Thrice, was nice.

Sixth period was this class called self-sustained silent reading; there we read. Every other month, the instructor took us to a big room, and we got to pick a book donated by Reading Is Fundamental.

Most got books like *Ripley's Believe It or Not* or *Guinness Book of World Records*. (Like they really needed to know how big the world's largest tapeworm was.) With my extra change, I'd often buy used classic books. Things that sounded good. Things that sounded smart. Things like *Notes from Underground* or *Wuthering Heights*. I usually read only the first chapter. Nevertheless, when I grow up, I'd like to have a whole room devoted to books. A library, like in that board game Clue.

Last period was Mr. Mirabelle with his overbite and droopy eyes. He stood in the front of the room drawing on the blackboard: atomic configurations and chemical bonding. There was only one chemical I wanted to bond with, so my imagination often took a detour: Demetrius. *Oh, Demetrius.* If I licked my lips long enough, I could taste him. Delicious Demetrius. He was so hypnotic. The way he walked. The way he dressed, always in the latest fashion. He was so classy, right down to his shiny socks.

After class, I followed him to his locker, thinking of that sports motto "You miss 100 percent of the shots you don't take."

"Demetrius!" My voice squeaked a little.

He turned my way. Understand, that was the closest I had ever been to him. His dreamy eyes and his liquid dark skin and those pearly white teeth . . .

I swallowed and continued. "Hello. I would just like to welcome you to Dardon Junior High."

Demetrius gave me an up and down and said, "Thank you." Then he walked away.

My chest heaved, and I giggled. Finally, I had at least made a connection.

I got home to see someone doing my job. Platform-shoed Horace parted the sheets, then folded them. I saw Ma behind him, tutoring (nagging) him in the fine art of domestic engineering. Ma was intolerant of ill-folded sheets and shirts that were not stupendously ironed. After she left, I asked Horace what was going on.

Horace sighed and told me, "I've been demoted to a woman."

I hit him with a towel.

"After this week, basic should be a breeze," Horace said.

"Daddy was maaaaaad at you," I said.

"Maine, you just heard it. I heard it and saw it."

"Was that vein popping out right here?" I pointed to my forehead.

Horace threw his head back in laughter. "Yes, yes."

"Good thing you're going into the service; you're

gonna have Daddy on blood pressure pills. Why did you steal a car anyway?"

"I didn't steal the whole Pinto, just the hubcaps. It was a dare. The guys were in on it too. We did it to be stupid."

"It was stupid all right."

"It was just a prank, Maine. Didn't you ever want to do something that was totally nuts?" he asked.

I thought for a minute, then answered, "No."

"Well, that's because you're the good one. The smart one. Now that I'm going away, it's up to you to hold things together," he told me.

"Me?"

"Yeah, you're the oldest now."

I frowned. "I think I saw this episode on *Bonanza*. I don't want to be Hoss. I want to be Audra."

"That's *Big Valley*," he corrected.

"I know. I just want to be the girl. The girl is never responsible for anything."

"This is nineteen seventy-five." He picked up the laundry basket. "You're liberated now."

"I'm liberated? What about you?" I asked. "This is the first sheet you've folded in seventeen years."

"Charmaine," I heard my mother call from upstairs.

I ran to the steps. "Yes, ma'am."

"Come with me to pick up Tracy John."

William B. Evans Elementary was a five-minute walk from our place. Ma's pace was so brisk and purposeful that she cut the time in half. We walked past dogs, bicycles, tricycles, unpretentious American cars, and small to moderate-sized houses in a blur. Her eyebrows were knitted with worry.

"Ma, am I what you'd call a late bloomer?"

She didn't even tip her head in my direction. "Child, you ain't but fourteen."

"Almost fifteen. I'll be fifteen in four months, and you were married at fifteen, remember?"

"That was different; that was the South."

"It's not that different. There's this new boy who just moved into the neighborhood. His name is Demetrius. Demetrius McGee."

"Charmaine, I have to concentrate on one thing at a time. I am going out of my ever-loving mind with Tracy John."

"What did he do?" I asked.

"Fight."

"Who is he fighting?"

"You know the Pembertons' boy."

I knew the Pembertons. They lived on Orchard Avenue. They were all brown skinned and had large heads. Mr. Pemberton drove a truck for Coca-Cola. Mrs. Pemberton was a stay-at-home ma like my ma was. Ralph was their only child so far.

On a bench outside the classroom, Tracy John had mastered the art of widening his penny-colored eyes. He knew how to enhance his soft child's features for full benefit. His skin looked so soft and buttery.

He didn't have a scratch on him. I wondered what Ralph looked like.

"You two wait here while I talk to Miss Mullins," Ma said.

Fuming, I watched her walk away. What, did she invite me down here so I could sit next to him?

"Why did you punch Ralph Pemberton?" I asked Tracy John flat out. Why make small talk here when we never really spoke at home?

Tracy John said nothing.

"Not talking? Then I'll find out some other way." I got up and ambled over to the door. I put my ear to the oak. All I could hear were murmurs, ghosts of words. Frustrated, I decided to go back to the bench. I turned and backed up into Tracy John's feet.

"Go back to the bench and sit," I told him.

"Go back to the bench and sit," he told me.

"Go back to the bench and sit," we said at the same time.

"Go." Our words clashed again.

"Right now." One more time.

He was really good for his age. I took another step back, grudgingly admiring his artistry.

I saw shadows approach the door.

Tracy John and I scrambled back to the bench and tried to look normal. I stared at the wall. Tracy John peered at the ceiling.

"Thank you very much, Miss Mullins. You will not have this problem again," Ma told the teacher quietly. Ma was like the godfather, quiet in speech, but forceful in tone. During the walk home, I expected her to say something stern to Tracy John, but she didn't.

By the time we got back to the house, Horace had made all the beds and had even spread a shawl at the foot of each one. Leo got back from dance lessons, his tap shoes slung across his shoulders.

When Daddy came home, I figured Tracy John was finally going to get it. I listened with my left ear and mashed a fork against the sides of the pan of gravy as Ma told him about her meeting with Tracy John's teacher. Flour lumps popped up like life preservers.

"She asked me if Tracy John's father was a white man," Ma said.

"What?"

"She asked if Tracy John was a mulatto."

"She's one of us, and she made that mistake?" Daddy exclaimed. I snuck a peek at his raised eyebrows; then I quickly turned back to the counter.

"She probably was comparing my color to his," Ma said. "I explained to her that Tracy John's mother had passed on."

"What did she say?"

"She said, 'Oh.' "

"Oh?"

"Yes, oh."

"What in the devil does this have to do with some schoolyard fight?"

"Tracy John won't tell what it was about," Ma said. "The teacher also said that he's very quiet."

"What in the hell is wrong with being quiet? This world could do with more quiet people. I'll tell you right now, this teacher ain't wrapped too tight. She's the one who ought to be checked out."

"She's young, Peyton. She looks like she's right out of school herself," Ma said. I was taken by how they both were so full of excuses for Tracy John.

Then Daddy called him. "Tracy John, get your little tan self down here."

Tracy John materialized promptly.

This ought to be good, I thought. At last, Tracy John was going to get what he deserved.

"Now, I know you know better than to go getting into trouble in school," Daddy began, but his voice had already softened. "School ain't no time for none of that funny business, you understand me? Now, you keep your hands to yourself." He gave Tracy John a little slap on his bottom, so quick I bet it didn't sting. "Get washed up for supper."

That's it? I wondered. *What bull!* That was the kind of stuff that made grass green. Manure. Or, as the French would say, *merde*.

I turned to see Tracy John walk away. He caught me spying on him, and he put his fingers in his ears and stuck out his tongue.

I glared at him as my eyes told him once and for all, *I declare war!*

Four

"I can't believe that Uppercase E would leave us holding the bag," Daddy moaned. "All he had to do was show up in court and face the music. One thousand dollars gone. Doesn't he know that we lose all the bail money?"

As I listened through the wall to my parents' bedroom, my eyes were stretched as wide as my ears.

"All he had to do was face the music," Daddy said.

"I'll clean houses, Peyton," Ma said. "I ain't proud."

"Well, I am. . . . I just can't believe I've been beat like this."

When Leo came upstairs, I waved him over. He took a space beside me against the wall. "They're talking about Uncle E," I told him.

"How are we going to meet the mortgage?" Daddy asked.

"Like I said, I'll step up my housecleaning. We'll make it," Ma said in her calm Alabaman way.

I was unable to contain myself; my eyes were bulging and my mouth was agape. Leo took my hand and led me away.

"How could this happen? Why would he do us like that?"

" 'Cuz he doesn't want to go to jail again, Maine," Leo said.

"You know we could be put out into the street?" I asked him.

"Daddy won't let that happen."

I hated Uncle E. He wasn't going to be happy until we were all in the poorhouse. He was the very definition of a two-bit criminal, forging checks to pay the water bill, shoplifting from Value City, getting caught with a nickel bag. . . . He had a scar on his left cheek like a stitched shoelace. He hardly ever shaved, leaving stubble like slivers of black ice. He was a year younger than Daddy but looked ten years older. Even worse, he behaved like he was *twenty* years younger.

I remembered how he had been released from jail to come to Auntie Karyn's funeral. Suited, this time shaven, but with a guard accompanying him. He was handcuffed, crying, and unable to wipe the tear from his eye or hold his little nephew.

•••

"Spread out there, y'all. Don't work tit to tit," Daddy told the boys. Horace, Leo, and Tracy John swept up the rubbish that careless people had thrown into our yard.

Daddy was really talking only to Horace, who was still on his bad side. It was the day before his ship date. Daddy went out every five minutes to oversee.

About his seventh trip to the yard, Daddy nodded approvingly as he surveyed the area. "That looks pretty good. Y'all come in for supper."

Horace's face lit up in surprise.

"Y'all didn't think I was gonna work you to death." Daddy winked at him. "Them days are over."

The boys ran into the house and scrubbed up for supper.

"That's a right good job you boys did out there," Ma said.

Tracy John sat up at the table. "Yeah, and this time we didn't work tit to tit."

Daddy, Leo, and Horace laughed.

"What did I say about that word, Tracy John?" Ma said.

He covered his mouth and tried to look innocent.

Ma had made Horace's favorite: beef tips and baked macaroni. For dessert, she brought out a double-layer yellow cake with chocolate frosting.

"Who is the cake for?" Horace asked hopefully.

All of us pointed at him.

The doorbell rang.

"That's the other part of our celebration," Ma said. "We asked your girlfriend over."

"Carol's coming over?" he asked, rubbing his hands together.

Ma looked at Daddy.

"No, Robin."

Horace's face dropped as he realized that our parents were perpetually on the wrong wavelength: Robin was so last month.

The doorbell rang again.

"Well, what are you waiting on, Horace? Get the door," Daddy told him.

Horace begrudgingly got up, throwing his napkin on the table.

Robin was a trip. Big shiny tears welled up between her lashes and trickled in long drops down her cheeks. "Horace," she called to him with her arms outstretched.

Horace swallowed, searching for the right words. "Robin," he finally said.

She said she would have loved to be over sooner but had been getting her hair done. And, boy, was it done, arranged in a princess style, bangs and a high ponytail. She bared her huge bright teeth, talking a mile a minute over cake and ice cream.

"Did you know that my father got me a job at Gimbels? Did you know that, Horace? Your girlfriend is going to be a career girl."

Horace just nodded and smiled.

"Are you gonna work in the shoe department like your father?" I asked.

"No." She leaned into Horace and squeezed his hand. "The confection department."

"That sounds important," Ma said.

I suppressed a roll of my eyes and the urge to correct my elders. Didn't Ma know that confection was just candy?

In the living room, Robin joined us to watch the family show *Sanford and Son*.

I didn't find Fred Sanford amusing at all. He'd berate his only son and call the sister of his departed wife ugly. George Jefferson of *The Jeffersons* was even worse. George was supposed to be rich, but he never did anything rich besides living in a penthouse.

If I was rich, I would invest in art. Exotic art. I'd have my pad looking like a museum. When other rich people came over, I'd pretend that I knew what everything meant.

Fred called Lamont a dummy. Horace laughed so hard that he had his legs in the air and was slapping the chair's armrest.

At nine that night, the sergeant called for Horace. He just wanted to touch base for the next day. I wondered how many recruits chickened out and didn't show.

Next, the bell rang. It was Mr. Clifford, Robin's father. He greeted everyone and told Robin to get her coat.

Daddy told Horace to get off the phone and say goodbye to Robin properly.

"I hope you become the most decorated soldier ever, Horace," she said, and gave him a frank kiss in front of all of us.

"Thanks, Robin. You take care too. I hope the candy counter treats you right," Horace said.

Not the most romantic words of parting I'd ever

heard, but it fit. I looked at Ma, and she was tearing up. But I knew that this was nothing like the waterfall that would ensue at O-dark-thirty the next day.

•••

Horace's recruiter, Sergeant Tay, was a six-foot-six, 236-pound Samoan. Though I wasn't into his military look, I had to hand it to a man who could look pulled together so early in the morning.

Daddy said he felt that Horace was in good hands with that "good-haired brother" seeing to him.

"Now, be sure to call us if things don't go right, you hear?" Ma said.

"It'll be all right, Ma," Horace said.

Ma wore the same worried look she'd had when she had gone to get Tracy John from school. It was just like a movie. In my mind, the soundtrack music swelled. The chorus sang its *ahhhhhahhhhhhhahahahaohhhhhhh*.

Horace, Claude, and Sergeant Tay drove off in an aqua Ford with a GO ARMY! license plate. They disappeared into the darkness as we waved and yawned and sniffed back our tears.

"Well, y' all go back inside and grab some shut-eye. You don't have to be up for a while," Daddy told us.

The house's only illumination was a soft, rich yellow kitchen light. I was still in my nightgown, but the thought of going back to sleep didn't appeal. Though I didn't have a real close relationship with my older brother, you get used to seeing a person every day and you miss him when you know that you won't see him anymore.

Ma put on a pot of coffee, and Daddy pulled up a chair at the table.

Ma started scrambling eggs. I helped her, putting butter in the pan.

The boys wore mopey faces. The trio had been severed, and the duo of Leo and Tracy John just scuffled around like they didn't know what to do with themselves. Finally, they joined Daddy at the table.

"Buck up, all of y'all," Daddy said in his round, deep voice. He patted Leo and Tracy John on their heads and looked at me and winked. "That's a part of growing up. You have to leave the nest. You have to spread your wings and fly." Daddy made bird noises and flapped his arms, but even that didn't change the boys' faces. "Soon it'll be just me and Miss Sweet Thang. All y'all will be up and grown."

Ma poured him coffee and made the boys hot chocolate. They still looked forlorn.

"All right, y'all, damn. Y'all knew this day would come," Daddy said.

"How come Horace has to leave so early?" Leo asked.

"Ain't no such thing as an afternoon army."

"Are they gonna take him out to the rifle range?" Leo asked.

"They ain't gonna do much with him the first day. Today is just to get settled. He'll meet people from all over the country. People come all the way from California."

Daddy smiled. My father had the best smile. It made the rest of the room fade into the background.

Ma and I set down steaming plates for them.

Tracy John just looked his over. "Does Horace get breakfast in the army?" he asked.

"Course, can't start the day on a cold stomach. He'll get lunch and dinner too," Daddy said. "Three hots and a cot."

• • •

Just as I was about to head out for school, Ma emerged from her bedroom in a pair of black heels, sheer nylons, a black skirt, and a standard white blouse.

"Where are you going dressed like that?" I asked.

She cut her eyes at me.

"I mean, where are you going so dressed up?"

"I got a job as a receptionist."

"I thought you were going to step up your house-keeping."

"This is more steady," she said. "I just have to answer phones. I get off at four-thirty. You be sure to look after Tracy John till I get home."

"Wait a minute. Wait a minute. You mean I have to watch Tracy John?"

"I don't have a minute, Charmaine." She refolded a bus schedule and put it in her purse.

"Why do I have to watch him?"

"Because I told you to."

"But—but—but—"

She left me to my buts. My confusion. And, boy, was I ever confused. Everything was moving so fast all of a sudden. I couldn't picture Ma at work in a world of beige carpets and light fixtures. I couldn't see her in a building twenty-five stories high.

My head was spinning.

Horace was in the army now.

Uncle E was on the lam.

Daddy was out a grand.

And I had to watch Tracy John.

●●●

Nosy and chatty, Cissy and Millicent went home with me that day to help with my task. Watching him color, pinching him, goo-gooing at him, they sat at the kitchen table with Tracy John. Unlike most kids, Tracy John didn't seem amused by lots of attention.

"Did you have a good day at school, Tracy John?" Millicent asked.

"I guess," he said.

"Did you learn anything fun, Tracy John?" Cissy asked.

"No," he said.

"What's your favorite subject, Tracy John?" Cissy asked.

"Gym."

"Oh, you like to play," Millicent said, and pinched him. "What do you want to be when you grow up?"

"A football player."

"Really? What team?" Cissy asked.

"Dallas."

"You're gonna be a Dallas Cowboy!" Millicent exclaimed.

"You would make a cute Cowboy, Tracy John," Cissy said.

"Oh, you would be adorable," Millicent said.

They continued pinching him and otherwise smothering him with affection as if they'd never seen a child before.

After they left, Tracy John eyed me warily, like a fox.

"Do you have something to say?" I asked him.

His penny brown eyes studied me a minute longer; then he said, "Your friends are boring."

"What?" I asked. "They aren't even good out the door."

"They are."

"What? They have always been very nice to you."

"They're still boring as hell."

"What did Ma tell you about cussing?"

"Boring as hell!" he sang, pronouncing *hell* as *hail*.

"Stop cussing."

"Hell. Hell. Hell," Tracy John said, drawing up proudly.

"You are so fresh. You are going to get your little butt cut." I paused to let this warning set in.

But he only got bolder. "Give me a glass of milk," he demanded. Then he had the gall to snap his fingers.

Shocked, I stuttered, "Y-y-you must be crazy. I'm not getting you anything."

Tracy John smirked, folded his arms, and said, "Boring as hell."

"That's it." I threw down the apron I had on. I had

42

been trying to look like Ma. "I'm sending you to your room."

"You can't do that. You ain't Auntie."

"Well, I'm doing it." I got my neck to going and my finger to pointing at the staircase. "Go up to your room."

"You go up to your room." Tracy John got his neck going just as sassy. He rolled his eyes and popped his hips.

"Go to your room," I said.

"Go to your room," he said.

"Go," we said at the same time.

I took a step back; we clashed again. "Go," we said at the same time.

Then I figured I'd flip up on him and change my words. "Right now," we said at the same time.

Dag, he was good. In the interest of time, I decided to call things a draw, but as I walked away I told him, "Just stay out of my way for the rest of the afternoon."

"Get me my milk, then."

I took a deep breath to contain myself.

"Get it," he told me.

I sighed again, and before I knew it I was pouring milk into a plastic cup and handing it to him. He took it without a thanks, without anything.

The silence stretched out as he walked away, and my eyeballs shot daggers at the back of his head.

• • •

Ma had made a concoction with onion, garlic, and mustard greens. She had also made stuffed bell peppers and black-eyed peas in molasses. All I had to do was warm it up. Since it was almost five and I had the table set, I figured I could get everything toasty for when Ma, Daddy, and Leo got home.

After I had everything on the stove, I spoke to Millicent on the phone.

There was a knock at the door.

"Someone's at the door? Who could that be?" I asked Millicent, and excused myself.

I opened it to find a figure about three-feet-something tall and fifty-something pounds. High yellow. With big copper-colored eyes.

"Tracy John, what the . . . ?"

He laughed and skittered by me like a mouse. The next thing I knew, he was in the living room, playing the stereo loudly, dancing about and clapping his hands and shaking his butt. He had it tuned to the rock station and was dancing to Led Zeppelin.

I followed him, shaking my fist. "You don't leave this house without asking me first."

He jumped on the furniture.

"Get off that couch!" I told him.

He was twisting and turning, acting a natural fool.

I went to grab him, but he moved, so I ended up holding on to air. I made another attempt, but he was too fast.

"Will you stop? Stop it!" I yelled at him.

All of a sudden, he did. "What smells?" he asked.

I inhaled deeply. Something did smell. Something smelled a lot like burning greens.

I ran into the kitchen only to find it full of smoke.

I removed the pans from the burners and turned off the gas. As I forked through the charred remains, I mourned what Ma had spent the morning preparing. I was close to tears.

Tracy John shook his head. "All you had to do was warm it up."

"Why don't you shut up? This is your fault."

"Oh, no it ain't. I wasn't talking on the phone."

"If I wasn't chasing after you every five seconds, maybe I could keep my mind on what it is I'm supposed to be doing."

"What are we having for supper?" he asked. Just when I thought if he said one more word I'd strangle him, he continued with "I don't want to starve. What are we going to have?"

My hands trembled with rage as they approached his turtlenecked throat.

The back door unlatched.

I pulled my hands away and put them behind me.

Ma came in, waving her arms and coughing from the smoke. "What in the world has gone on here?" she asked.

"I was just playing the radio," Tracy John said, running to Ma's side and squeezing her thighs.

"The radio?" she asked.

"Yeah, I was just listening to the radio. I don't know what was going on in here," Tracy John said.

"Why don't you shut up?" I said.

"Tracy John has a right to talk," Ma said.

"That's right, I can talk," Tracy John said.

I lunged at him. To stop me, Ma cast a stern eye.

Just then, Leo the tap-dance kid came in doing the shuffle off to Buffalo.

"It's kind of smoky in here, ain't it?" Leo was Captain Obvious. "How did everything go today?"

"Maine tried to lock me in my room," Tracy John said.

"I did not!" I screamed.

"She can't lock me in my room, can she, Auntie?" Tracy John asked.

"Don't believe a word he says," I said.

"I'm afraid of the dark," Tracy John said.

"You have lost your cotton-picking mind," I told him.

"And she didn't even help with my homework," Tracy John persisted.

I was furious. "You didn't tell me you had any!"

"It's not that far off that he'd have homework after coming home from school," Leo said.

"You're a manipulative little brat," I said to Tracy John, putting my hands on my hips. I turned to my mother. "He doesn't want to share; he wants to take over."

"Charmaine, get your hands off your imagination. I have never heard such foolishness in all my life," Ma said. "I asked you to do simple things, Charmaine. Heat up supper and watch Tracy John."

"Simple? Simple? I have *never* worked this hard in my life!"

Ma put on her apron, tying it around her waist and covering her business attire. "I don't want to come home after work and find this disarray."

"He is the devil's child. I sleep with one eye open," I whispered to Leo as I left the room.

46

"Don't prevent you from snoring none," Leo called after me.

•••

That night, I heard Leo down the hall washing his face and hands. I figured I'd take another shot at getting him on my side.

"You know what Tracy John said to me? He said Cissy and Millicent were as boring as hell."

"Your friends *do* get a little boring. Especially Cissy. She never says anything interesting."

I frowned. Like Leo's friends were so spectacular. He hung out with these kids from his dance class, and that was all they talked about: dance. But I didn't want to get on that. I would not be distracted. "Tracy John said the H word."

"So?"

I followed Leo into our room. "He said it a couple of times."

"And?"

"Pretty soon, he's gonna say D and maybe even S. Then M."

"M?" Leo asked.

"Yeah, M.F."

Leo put his shoes on the floor and his robe back on the hanger. "Maine, you're acting like an A-hole."

"Daddy created a brat," I said. "Daddy used to sit him on his lap and teach him all those words and tell him to run in to Ma."

47

"Turn the record over."

"He's spoiled."

"He's the youngest."

"He gets everything."

"Maine, get over it. You know Uncle E stiffed us. It's not Tracy John's fault. For Pete's sake, we'll all have to make sacrifices."

"He's bad. I don't mean bad meaning good; I mean he's bad-bad," I explained, but Leo had already rolled over and put a pillow over his head to block out the light and my words. "You're not even listening, Leo. I need your help. Do you really have to go to dance class? Can't you watch him Mondays and Wednesdays?"

He sat up. "I'm already set to watch him Tuesday, Thursday, and Friday."

"You said yourself everyone has to make sacrifices, Leo."

"I can't take off now. We're just about to learn an important step. We're just about to learn the shimmy sham."

"That's what I'm talking about, Leo. I'm getting the shimmy sham."

With that, Leo stood up, walked to the wall light, and flicked it off. It took me forty minutes of tossing and turning to get to sleep.

● ● ●

Ma wasn't a bra-burning woman who wanted to explore herself. No. My ma worked to make ends meet. I tried to articulate this to Cissy and Millicent.

"I don't know how much longer I can take this."

"I don't see why you're making such a big deal about this. My mom works," Cissy said.

"Yeah, but you're different. You don't have anyone to watch."

"Tracy John's not a problem, Maine. He's adorable," Millicent said. For lunch, Millicent always brought what everyone considered weird food: lox on a bagel.

"He's so lovable looking." Cissy was eating two sandwiches from home along with french fries she had purchased. She twirled one around in ketchup on her plate.

I thought of Tracy John's chubby lips, his tiny flared nostrils, his large doelike eyes, and of course, that buttery skin.

Objectively, he was a cute kid.

Subjectively, he was a pain in the butt.

"I wish I had a little brother," Millicent said.

"He's not my brother," I said, and got up from the table just as the bell rang for Mr. Gowdy's class.

Life was awful. Simply awful.

Wednesday was a mere twenty-four hours away. I'd have to do it all over again. Tracy John would put me through all that grief: insulting my friends, cussing, ringing the doorbell, dancing on the sofa, making me burn the greens.

● ● ●

That afternoon, I quickly learned that Leo was just as bad as Tracy John. I walked in, and they were both yukking it up on the telephone. They were crank-calling Ma and parroting her greeting.

49

Leo said, "Integrity Insurance Agency. Auto. Home. Life. Health. Business. Low down payments. Low monthly payments. May I help you?"

Then he hung up and the boys fell all over themselves laughing.

Tracy John pulled on Leo, saying, "Call her again. Call her again."

Leo began dialing.

"And talk like you're from the South," Tracy John said.

They laughed harder at that.

Ignore it, Maine, ignore it. . . .

"How's this," Leo said to Tracy John. "Inteeeeeegriddie."

"You sound like that guy on Bugs Bunny."

"Foghorn Leghorn."

"Yeah."

They laughed some more.

"Why don't you two jugheads quit bothering Ma at work?" I said, and took the phone from Leo's hands. I was convinced that Tracy John was corrupting Leo, because I was sure he wouldn't act that silly on his own.

"Boys, now, you know better than to play on the phone," Ma said, not knowing that I had picked up.

"They won't bother you again, Ma," I said.

They both looked at me like I had three heads; then they ran away.

What next? What else would they get into?

Five

The next day, my life got worse, or as the old folks say, worser.

I saw it, and my heart stood still.

In the cafeteria, my Prince Charming, my Demetrius McGee, with all his chocolate allure, was cozying up to Dinah Coverdale at the long-haired girls' table.

She was leaning into him, and he was feeding her his dessert. She was eating his Ring Ding.

How could this happen? He, my Demetrius, was lost in an image. That doggone Dorothy Dandridge look, that barely black look that was so celebrated. And there I was, still with midnight skin that I'd earned after only a few hours of summer outdoor activity. This color clung through hazy mid-September heat. It was still with me now in October. I hated it. I hated Dandridge. I mean, why was she an idol? Just because she was beautiful. The woman was dead at forty-two, either of a drug overdose or a broken foot. Something about a bone fragment swimming through her system, creating an aneurysm. She and Lena Horne could both go to hell.

By this white, approximated, quasi-European standard, I knew I was not the best-looking person. Frankly, I didn't even want to be pretty. I just wanted to be loved. I wanted the perks of prettiness.

I was sick and tired of these Lena Horne look-alikes getting everything while I stood around empty-handed.

Life is so physical. So based on how we look outside. And being a black girl who looked like a black girl, I felt, at times like these, well, shortchanged.

●●●

"Tracy John, do you have homework to go over?" I asked, letting the words go over hang.

And they hung. Tracy John didn't pick them up.

He said nothing.

"Oh, I see you're doing that too-cute-to-answer-me bit again."

He looked at me like I was crazy.

"Well, do you?" I asked.

Nothing.

"You are impossible. You know that?" I told him.

"I don't want to do my homework with you," he said.

I ignored him and pulled his schoolbook out of his backpack.

"Gimme my book," he said.

"Tell me what your homework is."

He begrudgingly showed me the page of the story his class was studying. I brightened to see that it was a military story; it made me think of Horace. I got him started on it, and soon we were sailing along pretty well. I was listening as he read. His chubby fingers eased across the page. His voice was remarkably fluid, given his age. Everything was everything for a good five minutes until that word came along. The word was *said*.

I corrected his pronunciation. "It's not *sade*. It's *sed*."

"I don't see no *e*," Tracy John snapped at me.

"You don't have to see an *e*. I'm telling you that is how that word is pronounced."

"I don't see no *e*." He got louder.

"You don't have to see no *e*."

"I don't want you to help me with my homework," he said, taking his book away from me. "You're mean."

"I'm mean?" I asked.

"Did I stutter?" he asked.

"Give me back that book."

"No."

"No? Now, see here. You don't say no to me. I'm supposed to be in charge of you. I'm supposed to be helping you with your homework. Now, give me back that book."

"No."

With that, I lost it. I stuck him with my pen. It wasn't as dramatic as it sounds. I had the cap still on it, and I poked him in his middle where he had some padding. Still, his eyes connected with mine with a scream that I was sure could have alerted the town's volunteer firemen.

Ma entered from the back door. She always managed to catch things at their worst. "Charmaine!" she exclaimed.

●●●

All that evening I had to listen to Ma's doting on Tracy John, her telling him "I don't see a mark there, dear," and her endless kisses to make it better. I was surprised she didn't take him to the emergency room to get him fitted for a cast.

As I got into bed, Leo said, "You shouldn't have stuck him with a pen, Maine."

"The cap was still on!" I snapped at him, then wondered aloud, "Why can't Uncle E take Tracy John in?"

Leo looked at me sharply. "Uncle E? You've got to be kidding. He's a freakin' fugitive. Who knows where he is?"

"What about Uncle O, then?"

"He just got divorced."

"So? He can take care of a kid. Tracy John can start off his family. He could be a single dad."

Leo rolled his eyes.

"Leo. What are we going to do?" I shook my head.

"We? What do you mean 'we'? I like Tracy John. So does everybody else. You are the only one with the problem."

"Fine. I'll be alone. I'll be that lone voice in the wilderness, like Gandhi."

"Nobody knows who you're talking about."

54

"Mahatma Gandhi led the fight against the caste system when India was a colony of Great Britain."

Leo just rolled his eyes again. "You know, that is so fascinating."

I growled. "It's Tracy John or me."

"Bye."

"Bye?"

"Yeah, give me a call when you get set up in your new place," he said in a tone that was no-nonsense, final, and irrevocable. He turned off the light.

I rolled over and clamped my eyes shut.

I decided right then: I hated all men. You just couldn't trust them. They stuck together like rice in a pot.

●●●

The next morning, I learned that women weren't any better.

"You have to be very patient with Charmaine," I overheard Ma saying to Tracy John.

"I am very patient, Auntie. She poked me with a pen."

"Tracy John, you are going to have to try even harder to be not only patient but also understanding. She is going through a change."

"What is she going to change into?"

"A young lady."

"What is she now?" Tracy John asked.

"She's in between a girl and a young lady."

"She's a teenager."

"That's right. And this is a very, very difficult time for her, so you have to promise me you will be understanding and patient and I won't have any more problems when she's watching you."

"Yes, ma'am," Tracy John said.

I stood at the door, deep in bewilderment. A vein was throbbing in my temple. I began to pace up and down. I restlessly sighed, wandering back into my bedroom.

So that's what Ma thinks of me.

Six

Thursday evening, I was stuck helping Ma with supper. I told her, "You know, Ma, there's a lot of prejudice here in Dardon."

"I don't see how that's possible, Charmaine. Ain't but two white families left here."

"I'm talking about black prejudice, Ma. Black on black."

"You're talking about what, now?" she asked me.

"Black on black. You know what this one girl, Dinah, said to me? She said she would have to take about ten trips to Jamaica back to back to look like me."

"What's that supposed to mean?"

"You know what that means, Ma."

"People say a lot of things that don't make no good sense," Ma told me, draining a can of salmon.

"I'm the darkest person in this family," I told her, chopping the onion.

"No, you ain't; I am. Since you want to get down to

shades," she said, looking over her shoulder. "And don't make those chops so big. How's anyone going to eat that?"

"I'm talking about the children," I said.

"I need another spoon."

I went to the drawer and handed my mother a long silver spoon. "Not only am I too dark, I am too skinny."

"I need the other spoon."

I went to the drawer again and took out the long wooden spoon. Walking back to Ma, I put one hand on my hip. "Here!"

"You better get your hands off your imagination," she told me, and she combined the salmon with onions, bread crumbs, mashed potatoes, eggs, and black pepper. "Pat," she told me.

I didn't.

"I said pat!"

Begrudgingly, I patted, my chin held high, hard, and straight. It was useless trying to communicate with her. She was a stone wall. I divvied the mixture into balls and shaped them into patties; then we coated the patties with cornmeal.

"You'll fill out. That I guarantee," Ma said. "Your color's yours to keep."

Daddy came in from the bright early-November sun.

"How's my two favorite girls?" he asked, giving me a quick squeeze, Ma a longer one.

"Peyton, please tell this young lady she will fill out," Ma requested.

Daddy looked me up and down and gave his hundred-watt smile. "Nope, Charmaine'll have those horse legs forever."

On an ordinary day, that might have been funny. That was not an ordinary day. Lately, none of my days had been ordinary.

Uncle O was over without his ex-wife, whom he was dating again. I wondered if they were having problems so soon. At the dinner table, I was still sulky. Daddy nudged me. "Aw, come on now, Miss Maine; if you can't make fun of a bony girl, who can you make fun of?"

Leo placed his hand over his mouth and nose to smother his laughter as his head bobbed.

Daddy saw this and pointed at him with his soup-spoon. "Leo's bony; you don't hear him squawking."

Leo blurted out, "She's not mad just because she's skinny. She's mad because she's black."

The room got very heavy. I mouthed to Leo, "I'm going to get you."

"All we have is our melanin," Uncle O proclaimed, then gestured at Tracy John. "Some of us don't even have that."

"Hey, black people come in every color from chalk to charcoal," Daddy said to his brother, patting Tracy John on the head lovingly.

I failed to see the collectiveness of this rainbow coalition. It seemed to me that the joys of black were not distributed equally. The near-whites like Tracy John and Dinah hogged them all.

Leo pointed at me with his fork. "You shouldn't be sorry that you're black; you should look forward to it every day."

"Yeah, cuz black is beautiful," Tracy John joined in, like he knew anything about it.

During a dessert of ice cream on a slab of cake, Daddy lapsed into a story.

"I must have been a year or two older than the peanut. I was riding my bike, and I took a curb the wrong way. I fell and I got myself tangled up in the spokes. This grown man walked toward me. I thought he was going to reach out his hand to help me up, but instead, he stepped over me. There I was, twisting and turning, trying to find my way out. Just as I broke free, I turned to watch that man walk away. And you know what I found out?"

"What?" we all asked.

"He was blind." He paused to let that set in.

"Did he have a stick? Did he have a dog?" Tracy John asked.

"He couldn't see my need. He didn't feel a need to help. He wasn't connected to me. He was blind. And I was blind to his blindness." He paused again, then said, "I don't want any of y'all ever, ever to be like that man."

Ma, Uncle O, and Leo nodded. Tracy John looked totally perplexed.

I grinned. A little boy couldn't possibly understand the complexity of that story. But I did. I understood that most people thought of themselves. Most people didn't really care about other people's well-being.

Dinah had stolen my love interest.

Uncle E had ripped us off for a grand. Now both Ma and Daddy were working nearly every hour that God created.

My auntie had loved a man who had killed her after promising us all that he wouldn't mess up anymore.

This was a no-good world filled with people who'd rather walk over you than help you.

•••

While buffing the rec room, Horace snuck us a call on the drill sergeant's phone.

"You're still holding things down, Maine?"

"Of course."

"How's your babysitting coming along?"

I didn't want to burden him, so I replied, "Just fine."

"Good. Little Tracy John's not hard to handle."

I opened up. "Are you kidding me? He's driving me up the wall."

"Maine, you're talking to a guy who spent the day digging with entrenching tools, pitching a tent, and digging crap holes."

"Crap holes?" I asked.

"Yeah, what do you think, they have a port-a-potty out in the war field?"

The intrigue of boot camp had worn off for me already. I was too wrapped up in my own problems to want to hear about his clothing issue, his growing personnel file, his second physical exam, and of course, the haircut. Even though he was soon going from white phase to red phase, M16s, M60s, and antipersonnel mines were nothing compared to watching Tracy John all afternoon.

On November 3, 1975, Mr. Mand wore a blue tie to

match his blue shirt. He lost control of his class. It was due to Walt Whitman's "I Sing the Body Electric." It was the "swimmer naked in the swimming-bath" phrase that got people laughing.

I liked the vers libre way Walt Whitman wrote. He seemed like such a wild spirit. And he had been an abolitionist, which scored him extra points with me.

Mr. Mand looked over the top of his glasses at us. "Now, class."

I was almost expecting him to call off class and drop the final curtain on this chaos.

Jumping in to provide order, I began reciting the remainder of the poem and pressed on until the rest of the class settled, reading it so that the syllables floated through the air above their nuttiness.

I gained full steam at the "Limitless limpid jets of love hot and enormous, quivering jelly of love, white-blow and delirious juice" line.

Out of the blue, another reader joined me. " 'As I see through a mist, one with inexpressible completeness and beauty,' " he said.

I turned to find out who was matching me in voice and articulation. It was only Spiderman (aka Raymond Newell). He had gotten his nickname for his double-jointed ability to wrap his legs under himself and walk on his hands. He hadn't done that trick since sixth grade, but the name stuck. He was as tall as I was, but skinnier (if you can believe that).

In our reading, we really had something going. Real

syncopation, like we had been rehearsing for a month. Spiderman, at the end, was standing, his arms stretched out to me.

He wasn't one for subtlety. I knew he liked me.

At the bell, I hurried from my seat.

"Charmaine," he called after me.

I turned reluctantly. "Hi, Spiderman."

"You want to go to the dance?"

I gave him an up-and-down look as the question registered. He was wearing the kind of clothes that made a skinny person look skinnier. Tight clothing, like a mime's. And those horrid colors, orange and green.

"You want to go to the dance with me?" he asked again, as if unheard the first time.

Though I wasn't into him, I never believed in being rude. "No, thank you," I told him, and walked away.

● ● ●

I wished black was white.

I wished dark was light.

I wished Demetrius had asked me to the dance instead of Spiderman. But he had asked Dinah.

The night of the dance, Uncle O came over with plans for miniature golf. Leo came up to the room to invite me and I told him unequivocally no.

"Why not?"

"I don't have time for that childishness."

"Are Millicent and Cissy coming over?" Leo asked.

63

"No, there's a dance tonight."

Leo examined my outfit: dungarees and a T-shirt. "You're going dressed like that?"

"I'm not going!" I screamed.

"What is your problem?" Leo asked, and left the room shaking his head.

Leo didn't understand anything. If my only choice was an unattractive date, then I'd have no date. I had so many goals and dreams; I couldn't settle. I walked into the hall and heard Leo and Tracy John conversing.

"Maine ain't coming?" Tracy John asked.

"No, she's in one of her moods again."

"But I like it when she comes. She doesn't let me win like you and Uncle O do."

"We won't let you win tonight, Tracy John."

"You promise?" Tracy John asked.

They shook on it.

"Maine is always moody, ain't she?" Tracy John said.

I walked to the edge of the room.

"I can hear everything!" I told them.

This time, both Tracy John and Leo stuck their thumbs in their ears, wiggled their fingers and stuck their tongues out, then ran away.

Around eight, Daddy's tired lips bent up at the corners when he saw me.

"How's my girl?"

"Great, Daddy," I said. I was on automatic pilot.

On Fridays he was always worn out. A few moments later, he was napping on the sofa, arms folded across his chest like he was in his final rest.

Ma was drawing a bath. They went to sleep at nine. For grown-ups, going to bed that early really wasn't going to bed. It was collapsing. That was the third week of her being a receptionist and a ma and a wife. It was taking its toll on her.

As for me, I just sighed and dreamed of the dance.

Were they playing Parliament? Could I have circled the edge of the dance floor to find him? Would I perhaps have been able to catch Demetrius's eye?

The soft sound of my sobs was muffled in my pillow.

Would I get more play if I wasn't the "smart girl"? Was that why boys ignored me? If I was giggly and flirty, could I attract more than Spiderman? What if Spiderman was the only boy who would ever be attracted to me? I just couldn't end up with someone like him. What would that look like? Two bony people together; we'd look like a pencil and a pen.

What's Cissy doing right now? Probably talking. She does talk a lot, lips moving like a young bird's. She's probably dancing too. Cissy was big, but she glided effortlessly in the latest dance steps.

Inhibited Millicent had all the coordination of a white girl on *Soul Train*, but she was probably dancing too.

By that time, if I had been at the dance, my hosiery would have run, and I would have seen about two straight hours of Dinah mashing against Demetrius. I had made the right decision in staying home.

I felt air as I pulled away my searching lips and cried some more.

Seven

On a scale of one to ten, the experience of watching Tracy John ventured into negative numbers, especially when I had to help him with his homework. Arithmetic was agony. Tracy John added five and two, and he put down eight.

"What's the right answer?" I asked him.

"Ain't that it?" Tracy John asked.

" 'Ain't' isn't a word. Say 'isn't.' "

"I can say 'ain't' if I want."

" 'Ain't' isn't a word."

He made that face I hated, baring his small, even white teeth as if he had fangs; then he clawed at me with his short fingernails.

Daddy entered. He saw the math book open and winked at us. Then his keen brown eyes surveyed the room in a rapid sweep. "Ain't Miss Sweet Thang home yet?" he asked.

Tracy John looked at me as if to say "What are you going to say to him?" I was tempted to wipe that smug look off Tracy John's face by saying to Daddy, " 'Ain't' isn't in the dictionary." But I restrained myself; as I said before, I was pro-life. I would *never* think of correcting Daddy.

Daddy left the room. Tracy John gathered his schoolbooks from the dining room table and followed him in a strut.

One-upped again.

•••

In U.S. history, we were discussing how the concept of free speech fit into the spirit of the civil rights movement.

"Congress shall make no law . . . ," Mr. Gowdy began, and he tossed his chin toward Demetrius to call on him.

My Demetrius had the newspaper out to the Phantom comics. He looked up.

Mr. Gowdy crossed his arms. "Demetrius, do you know which amendment I'm referring to?"

I was across from him with a row in between. There was an awkward gap of time in which Demetrius said nothing.

I had to help him out. I coughed, "First."

"First?" Demetrius asked me.

"That's correct, Demetrius. The First Amendment."

I saw out of the corner of my eye that he shot me a thankful look, and I flushed.

After class, he touched my shoulder. I hugged my chemistry book to my body to hide my flat chest.

"Thanks for what you did back there."

"Anytime, Demetrius."

"Really?"

"Sure."

He smiled. "Why don't you come over my house this afternoon?"

The earth stood still. I'm not exaggerating. I was going to have that magical pearly smile all to myself. "Would I like to come over your house? Is that what you're asking?"

"Yes."

"Yes?"

"Yes," he said. "So what's your answer?"

"Yes. Wait, no, I can't. I have to babysit. I have to watch Tracy John."

He turned to walk away, saying, "Some other time, then."

"Wait." I gulped air. "Tomorrow. Tomorrow. Please be free tomorrow. Are you free tomorrow?"

"Sure."

"Th-then i-i-it's a date," I said, stuttering, then laughing deliriously. I was that overjoyed.

• • •

Demetrius lived on the other side of Dardon, where a smattering of whites still dwelled. Where the dandelions and dirty cars weren't. I couldn't believe I was in his house.

"Where's Bobbie Sue today?" he asked me.

"Huh?"

"The little girl you watch?"

"You mean Tracy John." I laughed. "He's home. My brother watches him on Tuesday."

"Why don't you get a nanny?"

Nannies were in movies and on TV shows. I'd never seen one in real life. Nannies were like maids, and the only black person I'd ever seen with one of those was Mr. Jefferson. Like on that show, Demetrius had a Florence, but without the sass. Nondescript but purposeful. Over the course of the afternoon, I saw her actually do windows.

"Don't you have chores to do?" I asked, incredulous.

"No. That's what Daisy's for. Do you want a soda or something?"

"Sure."

"Daisy, can you get her a ginger ale?" He hailed her as if she was a taxicab. "You do such a good job, Charmaine. I watch you in class."

"You do?" I asked. My mind galloped. Did he see me when I wore my church dress? Did he notice that day when I snuck on lipstick in the girls' room and came to class alluringly red?

The maid/nanny brought the iced soft drink and put it on a felt pad.

"You know everything," he said coyly, and moved

closer to me. "I was wondering if you might be able to do my homework and sign my name."

I moved away from him. "You want me to sign your name?"

"Charmaine, please, it's just this little thing. It's just a paper or two. And the word problems in math."

"Eighteen sixty-five."

"What's that?"

"The year slavery was abolished."

He rolled his eyes. "Oh, come on, Charmaine."

"I'm supposed to just do your work for nothing, Demetrius?"

"Who says there's nothing in it for you? I think this is a great way for us to spend more time together."

What kind of fool does he think I am? "You're going out with Dinah."

"No, I'm not."

"I see you every day with her."

"I'm not with her now. Please?" he asked me.

"No."

"Please."

"No."

He stroked my hand. The next part was straight from a daydream: he pulled me in close, I leaned my head back, and he kissed me on my lips. *Yes!* I thought. I looked around at the chaise, the wine rack, and the vase with the Chinese characters on it. "Do you use a middle initial?" I asked him.

"No. Just write Demetrius McGee. Teachers don't know my handwriting yet."

Oh, Demetrius, I thought.

"Oh, Demetrius," I said.

That evening, before doing his trig homework, I practiced writing his surname with mine: *Charmaine Upshaw-McGee*.

• • •

The following day, I had to watch Tracy John, but the day after that, I was free to deliver my work to Demetrius's. I awaited my new assignment.

"You should have come yesterday; I had more work to give you. Doesn't your cousin ever go over a friend's house?"

"No."

"Why not?"

"Because he has no friends."

"No friends? What's wrong with him?"

"Nothing. He only likes certain people. He likes Ma and Daddy. He likes Horace and Leo. The rest of us inhabitants of the earth can just go flush ourselves. I don't think he wants to meet anyone new," I said, mimicking the way Tracy John squinched his face.

"Does he make that face when he meets new people?"

"He makes a worse face," I said, and squinched. We shared a moment. Me making faces. Him laughing. *Oh, Demetrius.*

"He's very particular about the people he associates with."

The phone rang, and Demetrius took it in another room.

I stood up, walked to the bookshelf, and copied down titles that struck me. I wrote down *Tropic of Capricorn* by

Henry Miller and *Gray's Anatomy*. Then I looked up and found the answer to my problem. He was austere and tall. He was striking, with high cheekbones and silky dark skin like Demetrius's. He looked far older than Tracy John, but I had a feeling he wasn't.

"How old are you?" I advanced toward him.

"Seven," the boy said.

I gripped his arm. "You're seven?"

"Ouch," he said.

"I'm sorry," I said, easing my grip on him. "Do you go to W. B. Evans Elementary School?"

"Yes."

"Your name?"

"Basil."

"Basil, you have to do me a favor."

• • •

I took a bright-clothes load down to the laundry section of the basement, hugging it to my chest. I was smiling and whistling as I worked.

"What's wrong with you?" Leo asked.

"I think I finally figured it out."

"Figured what out?"

"Cousin Tracy John."

"Yeah?"

I was grinning so much I could feel my eyes pinching. "I'm going to kill him with kindness."

"Say what?" Leo's eyebrows flew up.

72

I opened the lid on the washer. "Get this: I'm going to be so nice to Tracy John, it's going to blow his mind."

Leo seemed to lose interest.

"Did you hear me, Leo?"

He nodded and said, "That's what you should have been doing from the start."

• • •

"Did you tell some boy to talk to me?" Tracy John asked. His brow was furrowed.

"What's the boy's name?" I asked, and put down the pencil that I was using to configure Demetrius's math problems.

"Basil." I turned toward him. He studied my face.

"Basil, you say?" I asked.

"Basil McGoo."

"McGee," I corrected. "I did. Was he nice to you?"

"He asked me over his house tomorrow."

"Did Ma say you could go?"

He nodded.

"Then you have a new friend."

He had no answer to that; he just ran away.

"Yes!" I must have jumped three feet off the ground cheering.

• • •

73

The maid, who wore a severe expression, let me in. Did Demetrius's father treat her badly, or was she just a sourpuss? I guessed the latter. She showed me to the living room.

I sat there drinking in the resplendence of that house. My house was cozy and traditional and warm, but this house was modern and minimalist. Stark furniture. Primary colors. Overhearing voices in the kitchen, I got up and saw my cousin and Basil at the breakfast bar playing a board game that involved dice.

"Ain't Demetrius your brother?" Tracy John asked Basil.

"No, he's my half brother," Basil answered.

"Half? Split in half?" Tracy John asked.

"No, we have different mothers."

"And that makes y'all half?"

Basil nodded.

"Maine likes your half brother." Tracy John's voice was soft and insinuating.

"I know," Basil said. "A lot of girls do."

"What makes him so special?" Tracy John humphed.

Since I didn't like the turn of the conversation, I stepped from the shadows, saying, "Tracy John, it's time to go."

A few days later, Basil was over our house. Thankfully, they stayed outside and out of my way. They ran around the yard with a kite.

I looked out ten minutes after they'd started playing, and they had unhappy faces, their plump lips turned down, and their chins propped in their hands.

I went out to see what the problem was. They pointed at the tree. The kite was stuck on a limb that was six feet from the ground.

I reached for it; it was one of those rare moments when I wished I was taller, if only a few centimeters. I stretched and stretched, saying to myself, *I believe I can fly.* I looked back at them; they stretched their short necks, looking up at me very hopefully. When I stopped, they looked dejected and disappointed.

I went inside, and I came back outside carrying a prop.

"That's Auntie's favorite chair," Tracy John said.

I patted him on the head. "So we don't tell her." I told them both to brace the chair as I stepped onto it.

I reached the kite and untangled it just as Tracy John took his hand off his side of the chair. I tumbled right onto Basil.

Tracy John giggled.

I got up from the ground, totally incensed. I went at him, trembling with fury. "Tracy John, you did that on purpose. I could have split my head open falling like that, you—you—"

Only inches away from him, I remembered myself and my strategy. "You little dear thing, you," I said, and pinched his cheek.

After the maid/nanny came by for Basil, Tracy John came up to me with his hands on his hips, squaring off before me. "How come you're acting like this to me?" he demanded.

I used my innocent voice. "Like what?"

"Nice."

"I don't know what you're talking about," I said, inwardly grinning.

"Yes, you do!"

"No, I don't." This time I added a smile and called him sweet thang.

At that, a look of horror swept over his face, and he ran from the room. I broke out laughing. I just broke out. He'd looked at me like I was some unidentified flying object. I loved messing with his little mind. My fiendish plot was working.

Eight

"You're not going to get Demetrius. You're not gonna get anyone, as black as you are."

I knew the nasal, harping voice even before I looked up.

"He belongs to me," Dinah said.

"Girls." Our self-sustained silent reading teacher clapped her hands.

Dinah made like she was walking back to her desk, but then she added, "Besides, he doesn't like girls with flat chests."

Dinah was really talking out of her neck on that one. I hadn't seen her together with Demetrius since I'd gone over to his house the first time. Nevertheless, Demetrius gave me few signs of intimacy. But he sure kept piling on the homework. The only thing he was doing himself was his Spanish, since I was studying French. Still, I got to sit next to him on the patio, sipping a cola that the maid had fetched.

Demetrius sipped Mello Yello. "My dad likes you. He thinks you're wholesome."

"What do you think of me, Demetrius?" I asked.

"You're pretty smart."

"Anything else?"

"No, that's about it."

I frowned and changed the subject, asking Demetrius about the Maryland license plate on his father's Japanese car.

"We moved from Baltimore."

"Does your mother still live there?"

"My mother died in a car accident when I was fourteen months old," he told me.

"I'm so sorry." I took his hand. "Do you remember her?"

"Not at all."

I thought, *I hope Tracy John remembers Auntie Karyn.*

"He got remarried. Nurses shouldn't marry doctors." He spoke as smoothly as he always did.

"My auntie was a nurse," I said.

"He was only married a year or two. The judge awarded him custody."

"You went to court?" I cringed slightly. I'd thought that only white people went to court over their children.

"Yeah, the judge thought it would be better if we stuck together."

"Well, that's good."

"I don't care," he said, grinding his words, making them seem trivial.

"Yes, you do," I insisted. "Basil's your brother."

"Half brother, and no, I don't care. He should have stayed with his mother down in Baltimore. Dad doesn't have time for him. He wants to make head of surgery within the next few years."

"Still, what about you and Basil? Don't you ever sit with him and go over his homework?"

He rolled his eyes. "Oh, come on. I'm not his legal guardian."

I grinned. Who was I talking to? Demetrius didn't even want to do his own homework.

•••

Ma was totally against peewee football. She said it was too rough and Tracy John was too little. Tracy John begged and begged and begged to be on the team like Basil was. It's a funny thing about even the most stringent parents: you ask them for something one hundred or so times, and miraculously, they change their minds. Ma conceded that Tracy John could be in the club, but upon his first scratch, he'd be out.

Practice took Tracy John away from me on a consistent basis. One rainy day, however, I found myself home with him, and my patience was short. I was unused to him sitting at the table and to having to get him things.

"I want an apple," he told me.

After I had given him one, he said, "I like my apples sliced."

I took the apple to the counter and sliced it through the middle, then into quarters.

I handed it to him. "There."

He bared his would-be fangs and raked his would-be claws at me. Then he ate the snack and told me, "You cut it too big."

That sassy, confrontational monster. That turtle-necked, corduroy-pants-wearing, angel-faced little creep.

"Why don't you stop being so fresh and hardheaded?" I asked him, but he'd already run away.

He came back a few moments later with a basketball.

"Stop bouncing that," I told him.

"I'm not bouncing it. I'm trying to twirl it," he said, trying to maneuver it with his pudgy fingers, but it kept falling on the tile. "Horace can do this real good."

"Why won't you do what I told you?" I took the ball from him. "I'm not going to chase you every five minutes."

He tried to take the ball back, but I held it out of his reach. Then I put it in the pantry. "You are so spoiled. You don't know the meaning of the word *no*. You make me so sick and annoyed."

"Then why don't you leave?" he asked me.

I got right up in his face. "Why don't I—why don't *I*?" I stamped my foot. "You're the one who should go. They should have put you in the orphanage." No sooner did I air those looming feelings of resentment than I wanted to take them back. He looked like he was going to cry. "Tracy John, I'm sor—" I began.

Tracy John swung at me and connected with my left eye. My glasses went flying and landed in the sink.

"Tracy John, I'm sorry. I am. I didn't mean to say that."

He was still mad and swinging. I held his arm still. His nostrils flared, and his face was ruddy.

"Tracy . . ." I watched him stomp out of the room. My left eye didn't feel like mine.

Some kids get whoopings with their pants down or with a strap or a hairbrush or a limb from a tree. When Daddy got home, Tracy John got a spanking. Daddy put Tracy John on his knee and gave him ritualistic whacks with his bare hands. He said, "Tracy John, we tried to fight our way from getting on those ships. Then, when we were on the ships, we fought to turn them around. Then, when the ships docked, we fought so that we wouldn't have to get off. That is why the last thing we should ever do to each other is fight. We should love each other, damn it. Now, I didn't want to do that, but you have disappointed me." His words made the house shake, but that was only part one.

Part two involved me directly.

Tracy John wore a scowl of puzzlement.

"Is there something you want to say to Charmaine?" Daddy asked him.

He opened his mouth, then closed it, then opened it again. Then closed it. This was the same boy who had gone right into a boxing stance and jabbed out his right arm, connecting with its target, my face, just moments before.

Tracy John fixed his face the same way he did when he was eating beets. "No," he said. Then he said, "Yes." His face squinched up more. "I-I-I guess I-I'm sorry I hit you, Charmaine."

"Tracy John—" I began, but he ran away before I had a chance to finish.

"It was my fault, Daddy—"

"Charmaine, I don't care what you said; that boy has got to learn to keep his hands to himself, especially with women. Besides, no child ever got brain damage from a swat on the rear end." Daddy lifted the homemade ice pack (cubes wrapped in a washcloth) from my eye. "That boy's got a punch."

Who was he telling?

• • •

Later on that night, we heard a commotion on the stairs, and Leo and I sat up in bed.

Tracy John was going downstairs, lugging a full-sized suitcase. He headed straight for the front door, set the bags down, then began struggling with the doorknob.

Leo and I crouched by the stairs.

"What's Tracy John doing?" Leo asked me.

"What in the hell do you call yourself doing?" Daddy stood in front of Tracy John.

"I'm running away from home," Tracy John declared in his distinctive voice.

"Honey, what are you talking about?" Ma asked him.

82

"Tracy John, you are about to get your little butt cut. I'm not gonna take any more foolishness out of you tonight," Daddy said.

I ran downstairs, fearing that Daddy would take him over his knee again.

When I got to the foot of the stairs, Ma was asking Tracy John, "Do you know what's out there?"

"Bonsall Avenue," Tracy John answered quickly.

"Give me that." Ma took the bag from his hands and gave it to me.

I took it back upstairs to his room and opened it. I realized why it was so light. He didn't have anything practical in it, just a bar of soap, a towel, a football, and his piggy bank.

"You're gonna get in that bed, and you are going to go to sleep. Do you understand me?" Daddy told him. His voice boomed from downstairs.

As I put his piggy bank back on his dresser, Tracy John and Ma came upstairs. Tracy John said, "Don't touch my stuff."

Ma held him back. "She's just putting your things away," she said.

"I don't want her in my room," he said.

"I'm leaving," I said, exiting quickly.

● ● ●

The next day, I still felt terrible. During lunch I explained to Cissy and Millicent what had happened.

"That poor little thing," Millicent mourned.

"You shouldn't have said that to him," Cissy said.

"Take a look at my black eye," I told them.

"Put yourself in his shoes," Millicent said. "That little boy has had enough upheaval in his life."

"All everyone gives him is sympathy. What about me?" I asked.

"What about you? What do you have against you?" Millicent asked.

"I'm just perfect. Everything is swell."

Millicent nodded. "That's just what I said."

●●●

Sitting in maddeningly dry classes for the rest of the day was useless, like trying to eat spaghetti with a spoon. I held my eye, though it didn't hurt much anymore. This was nothing. I remembered one time I saw Auntie Karyn. Her bruises took on rainbow colors on the long bone of her jaw. A little blue. A little yellow. Auntie Karyn hadn't deserved what she had gotten. I wished she hadn't fallen for that man. If she hadn't, she would have still been alive. Strange, though—Tracy John wouldn't.

The bell rang, and I went down the hall to another class and on and on as if on a conveyer belt.

"I didn't know black people could get a black eye," Dinah said, and nudged me.

I was mad enough to grab her and throw her against the locker. Smash her head in a few times. Rake her on the pavement. Throw her in a garbage truck. Then dust off my hands. But as my trance of anger lifted, I found she was down the hall. I couldn't get to her even if I was still inclined. That was the traffic pattern of rush hour, and between periods it was gridlock.

Still, I hated Dinah. She had a boundless cruelty about her that there was no quenching.

I found myself in chemistry with Mr. Mirabelle scrawling figures on the board, everyone else in the room hopelessly scribbling things. Students copied but did not learn. At the bell, Demetrius handed me a list of items he wanted me to complete.

What was the point of life?

Why was I really on Earth?

●●●

At home, Tracy John continued with his showy anger at me. The way he looked at me was the way I looked at Dinah. I tried apologizing to him again, but he covered his ears and ran away.

I wanted things to be like they had been before he'd decked me. But when I thought about it, I realized that wasn't possible. My bruised eye would go away, but I had a feeling he'd be bruised inside forever from my ignorant comment. How could I have done a thing like that? How could I have given him what someone had given me— such a profound, oppressive, stabbing emptiness?

He didn't even want to come down for supper. He resisted Ma's coaxing, ignored Leo's request. Thank God for Daddy. Daddy didn't ask; he told.

"Tracy John, you better bring your little tan self down here!" Daddy called from the steps.

In double time, my cousin came front and center.

Daddy waved him on. "You come to the table, and you sit with your family."

Tracy John made a face. The only seat open was next to me.

"I don't want to sit there," he said.

Daddy shot him a look that could split wood. "You better sit your little happy behind down and break bread with us."

Tracy John looked my way and moved his chair away from me. He sat down cautiously.

The plates went around with candied sweets, string beans, and fried chicken. And the conversation was the usual mix: we wondered how the army was treating Horace and discussed current events. Tracy John ate without speaking. Not even with Leo. He didn't look up at anyone.

•••

After supper, Tracy John seemed much better. There was a game on, and he and Daddy watched it, cheering and jeering.

He came into the kitchen while Ma and I were washing dishes.

"Can I have a nice ice-cold beer?" Tracy John asked.

Ma craned her neck around.

"For Unc," he added with an impish grin.

86

I took a beer out of the fridge and opened it for him. He left without another word.

I peeked into the living room at them. Tracy John was on Daddy's lap.

"Ahhhhh, that's good." Daddy slurped the beer.

"Ahhhhh, that's good." Tracy John took a fake slurp.

"Ahhhhh," they said together.

Nine

I had been a recidivist.

In recidivism, a criminal reverted to his or her old ways of wrongdoing. That was the old me.

That night, I didn't sleep. Instead, I looked up at the moon and the stars, all the while hoping that God would help me understand. I thought hard about Auntie Karyn and came to the realization that she probably wouldn't like the fact that I couldn't get along with her own son.

The next morning, as Ma put concealer over my shiner (who knew she had makeup?), she told me to be sure that Tracy John brought home his rubber boots.

"I'm watching him this afternoon?" I asked her.

"Of course, Charmaine; what's changed?" she asked.

I thought for a moment and answered, "Nothing."

• • •

As I got home and took off my coat, the phone rang. Tracy John had been in a fight with Ralph Pemberton. So I put my coat back on and walked to the elementary school. There was frost in the air. The leaves were maple golden and crimson. Autumn was nearly over.

I entered the school, passing through corridors of rocket paintings, red, white, and blue.

Tracy John was alone on the bench. His shoulders were slumped like a defeated soldier's, and soft, delicate tears streamed down his face. He wiped them away when he saw me.

"Where's Auntie?" he asked.

"I'm Auntie today. You know that."

Tracy John looked away.

"You going to be okay sitting here while I talk to your teacher?"

He nodded.

I stepped into the room to find the well-dressed, efficient-looking Miss Mullins. She had on a beige dress with an A-line cut.

"You're not Mrs. Upshaw," she said to me.

"I'm Miss Upshaw."

"I need to see his guardian."

I pressed my lips together, thinking hard before answering. "Where's Ralph Pemberton's guardian?"

"I suppose they are at home."

"Why is that? Why is that?" I asked. "He should be here. He's the other party in this. We need to hear from all sides."

"Young lady, you are hardly in the position to speak to me like this." She stood up.

89

I was younger but taller. She was a pint-sized woman. I wasn't going to back down.

I said, "My mother put me in charge till four-thirty."

"I really shouldn't be telling—"

"I'm she. It. Me. Me. Me. Until four-thirty. It's me." I overtalked her.

"I have something very important—"

"Tell me, then."

She pointed at me. "Your cousin has a behavioral problem. And he's learning disabled."

"Learning disabled? My cousin?" My feelings hovered between anger and sadness. Anger was winning out. "Do you have any evidence? Do you have facts, or is this just your opinion?"

"I have a degree in education. I am going to recommend that Tracy John be sent—"

"I want to see evidence before you send my cousin anywhere."

"He obviously cannot conduct himself properly with the normal children in this class."

"My cousin is just as normal as anyone else, maybe more so," I told her, and yes, I did have my hands planted on my hips. "Can't you see that he's upset? Can't you see that Ralph has said or done something to upset him?"

"I really have to speak to Mrs. Upshaw."

"Why is Tracy John singled out?"

"I have to speak to your mother."

"Behavioral problems? Because he got in a fight?"

"This is the second time," she said dryly.

I closed my eyes, took a breath, and put on a ready smile that was wide, even, and precise. "My cousin has been reading since he was three and a half years old. He understands fractions and long division. So next time you want to label someone, you make it Ralph Pemberton. It's also his second time fighting with Tracy John. You'd better check him out!"

As I turned to leave, I saw that Tracy John was at the door, mute with amazement. He'd been listening all the time. I went into the cloakroom to get his coat, lunch box, rubber boots, and book bag, then took his hand and exited.

"You pack better for school than you did when you were about to run away," I told him.

"Auntie said it was going to rain. . . . I'm going to take these boots next time I run away," he said.

"What do you mean 'next time'? There's not going to be no next time."

"I'm going to stick my thumbs out on the side of the road. That's what they do in the movies," he explained.

I stopped walking. "You'd better be joking. You'd better not run away. I'd miss you."

"No, you wouldn't. You don't care about me."

"Then why do you think I stood up for you just now?"

"You like creating a scene."

"Tracy John, I care about you."

"You don't even like me. You hate watching me."

"No, I don't."

"Charmaine, I hate you!"

91

"Don't say that. You don't mean that."

"It's true. You ruin everything. Because of you, I can't go to practice. I got grounded and spanked," he said.

"I said I was sorry."

"I'm in more trouble than Horace was. He only got grounded, and he got in trouble with the cops."

"Horace is a little big to be put over Daddy's knee."

Tracy John's nostrils flared at that, and he asked, "Is Leo?"

I thought for a moment about my eleven-months-younger brother. "He's borderline. We'll see next time he acts up."

Tracy John frowned. "Leo doesn't act up."

I shook my head. "He has his turns. You just don't remember them."

"Do you have turns? Do you ever get a whooping?"

I nodded.

"When?"

"Plenty of times. Mostly before you were born. Other times you're too young to remember. Daddy doesn't play. Neither does Ma."

"If I was a parent, I wouldn't whoop my kids."

"Children have to have rules. You can't have your kids running the streets."

"The streets of Bonsall Avenue," he said.

That made me laugh a little. Dardon was hardly rough-and-tumble. "That's right: the streets of Bonsall Avenue." My voice softened. "Tracy John, you know, I didn't mean what I said. I was just frustrated. You were running around. Acting up. Not listening to me—but I didn't mean it. I know you don't believe me."

"I don't," he said. His light-complexioned face was tinted red in the high sun. For someone with such a sweet face, he had a hard way about him. I put down his gear by the gray metal swing sets and asked, "You want a swing?"

He took me up on my offer.

After a few good pushes that sent him soaring into the cool autumn air, he said, "I wish I had my own ma." I could tell that Tracy John was almost in tears. Angry and sad at the same time.

In my head, a dam broke. I stopped pushing him.

I managed to get out the affirmation: "You do."

Tears leaked out his eyes as he said, "No, no, she's not here. I'm an orphan."

Kneeling in the dirt, I wiped his tearing eyes, and then he said something that really broke my heart. "If you don't have a ma of your own, you could get sent away. Anytime they want to, they can get rid of me," he said.

"What? What makes you think that would ever happen?"

"They could," he said. "Just like you said."

"I said something stupid, Tracy John. I'm sorry," I said. "They wouldn't do that in a billion years."

Tracy John's clear round copper eyes welled tears; they slid down his puffy cheeks, wetting me. I held him in my arms.

I didn't have any tissue. Tracy John was a mess of tears and snot. The front of my blouse was soaked.

"Ralph called me an orphan."

"That's what you had the fight about?" I asked. I stroked the side of his face, trying to make him smile. "Tracy John—"

"I know, I know, keep my hands to myself," he said in a fuzzy voice that came from the tears in his throat.

"Well, that's true. But I was going to say something different. Tracy John, you shouldn't pay any attention to people like Ralph. They have wicked hearts."

He broke from my embrace and stood in front of me. He folded his arms and said, "I'm just like the girl from the comic strip with the red hair and the dog."

"Tracy John, you are nothing like Little Orphan Annie. You don't live in New York City. You live in Dardon, Pennsylvania. Some bald-headed millionaire is not going to come into your life and whisk you off to his mansion. The home that you live in is not large, but it has a backyard. Your auntie is afraid of dogs, so no Sandy for you. But you have a whole family who would do anything to see you smile. Including me."

I wasn't sure whether any of that was sinking in for him, but it was sinking in for me.

All that time, I'd never known that he missed his mother. Here I'd been feeling envious of him; I'd had no idea that he was hurting so deeply.

Before the first raindrop, I hugged him tightly and said softly, "Everything will be all right, Tracy John." After a while, we walked home through the driving rain.

Daddy had to work late, so he wasn't at supper.

Tracy John was very quiet, moving food around on the

plate, not eating it, like some fussy bird. Leo was going on and on about his mastery of the shimmy sham. He gave us the date of the spring concert, April 13. Tracy John stood up, walked over to Ma's seat, and asked her, "Auntie, can I be excused?"

"What's wrong, honey? Don't you feel well?" Ma asked, putting her lips to his forehead.

He didn't answer. I was looking at him, but he didn't meet my eyes.

"You go on upstairs; I'll be up to look in on you," Ma told him.

I watched him walk toward the stairs.

"Can I look in on him?" I asked Ma.

"Why do you want to look in on him?" Leo asked.

"Mind your business. . . . Ma, I know why Tracy John is upset."

"Why?" Leo asked.

I turned to him. "Are you Ma?" Then I went back to Ma. I was too incensed to mince words. "Miss Mullins is off her rocker. She wanted to put Tracy John in a special class. And Ralph Pemberton, ooooooh. Ralph Pemberton is an instigating jackass. He started fights with Tracy John. . . . I'm going to take him some dessert."

I went into his room carrying a bowl of bread pudding behind my back. The light was off, so the hall light was my only guide.

Tracy John was still in his day clothes, but he was beneath the covers.

"You're feeling better?" I asked.

He shook his head.

"You're feeling worse?" I asked.

He nodded.

"What would you do if I asked questions that required something beyond a yes or no answer?"

He shrugged.

"Do you think you'll be able to talk to me tomorrow?"

He smiled.

I took the bread pudding from behind my back. "You want some?"

He shook his head.

I took a whiff of the cinnamon. "You sure?"

He nodded.

I smiled and said, "I'll put it in the fridge. It'll be just as good tomorrow."

•••

While doing the dishes, I filled Ma in more. "Auntie Karyn wouldn't want him to be shut away in some class for kids who have behavioral problems. How's he ever supposed to go to college? Auntie Karyn would want him to go to college just like she did. Auntie Karyn did—"

Ma put the pots in the range rack. "Charmaine, Charmaine, take a breath."

"He shouldn't be left back; he should be . . . skipped."

"All right, Charmaine."

"Tracy John should be skipped. He reads well and knows fractions and long division."

"One thing's for sure," Ma said, drying her hands on

the red and white gingham apron, "we can't do anything about it now."

"Tomorrow, will you call and see?"

"You two are exactly alike. You're both so sensitive," Ma said.

"Tracy John can't go into that special class, Ma. It's all Ralph Pemberton's fault. All he does is pick. And nobody picks on my cousin." The phone rang. I added, "Except for me."

The phone rang again.

I ran to it, picked up the receiver, and said, "Upshaw residence." It was Horace. He had snuck us a call during his cleaning detail.

He told me that he was going out on the range the next day and that he hoped to shoot at least thirty-six out of forty, so that he might make sharpshooter. It occurred to me that he was breezing through things very competently. He told me that he had no weekend off and that going to the chapel each Sunday was his idea of an outing. I smiled, not because of what he was saying; it was just that his voice sounded good and strong and proud.

"Tonight, I have to pull fireguard," he said.

"Watch out for those pyromaniacs," I told him.

Ten

I overheard Ma and Daddy in the foyer the next morning.

"Woman, if you don't stop fussing over that little boy . . . ," Daddy said.

"Let me just—" Ma began.

"Woman, if you don't stop fussing over me . . ."

I went down to see Ma still straightening Tracy John's and Daddy's ties. They looked pretty spiffy, all dressed like it was Sunday.

It turned out Daddy had already called the principal and set up an appointment. While Ma paced and wrung her hands, Daddy radiated confidence. "We're gonna get all this worked out," he told us, and then they were off.

Tracy John just couldn't get placed in one of those behavior problem classes. They were like crime school. Kids there threw desks and used bad words in casual conversations. My poor little cousin couldn't thrive in that environment. Those boys would totally corrupt him. Next thing you knew, he'd be smoking. After Tracy John had spent a few weeks with those pint-sized delinquents, even Daddy would throw up his hands to him, because by that time, Tracy John would be carrying a knife or worse. Then they'd recruit Tracy John into some gang like the Dardon Knights, or the Wheels of Soul, or the local chapter of the Crips. He'd probably drop out of school.

I'd see him years later, and he'd be on heroin, living in a beat-up van, traveling the country with other misdiagnosed young men, all because of that confounded Ralph Pemberton.

By the time I got home from school, I had come to accept that Tracy John had been sweet when I had thought he was incorrigible, and that now he was going to have his sweetness extracted from him by this system, and he was going to be incorrigible for real.

Leo was in the back room with a friend of his. She was almost as tall as he was and had marcelled hair. They were practicing a dancè routine. They used their bodies as drums.

"Aren't Tracy John and Ma home yet?" I asked.

"Nope," Leo answered.

Dejected, I changed from my school clothes to my after-school clothes. I started on my chores. I finished the downstairs bathroom and began on the upstairs one.

"Where's Maine?"

I heard his voice, and I took off the yellow gloves just

in time for him to tackle me. He hugged me so tightly, he almost crushed my ribs. I returned the favor. I squeezed him back. He yelped, unable to speak.

I laughed. "You know what they say in church: take your time."

He took a breath. "Guess who's in the second grade?"

"Tracy John Upshaw?" I gasped. Now I was short of breath.

He nodded. "Second grade is so much better than first grade!"

"They moved you already?"

"This afternoon."

"No."

"Yes. I'm in Basil's class. And Richard and Hughie are in the same class as me."

I cheered. "From your peewee league!"

We hugged again.

"The beginning of this year, I didn't have any friends, and I hated school. Now I have a lot of friends, and I'm on the football team." His arms were stretched into the air. "Life is perfect. I love the world."

I shook my head. *Look at that smile—nice even white teeth, not barbed as fangs.* He was the cutest little thing in the world. He even asked me if I wanted some help.

"No, I can finish this all by myself. You go tell Leo."

"Thanks, Maine." He kissed me on my healing eyelid, then ran away.

Eleven

One day the following week, Ma was at work, Leo had tap, and Tracy John had peewee, so I had the whole place to myself. I could walk around naked, drink milk out of the carton, call Millicent or Cissy and talk for hours. I ended up not doing anything special because I heard an unexpected knock on the door.

"What are you two doing here?" I asked.

In the doorway, as Basil gave the reason, Tracy John was shivering. He sneezed twice. His warm brown eyes were glassy and watering. "Coach Albert sent him here. He said he was too sick to play," Basil said.

Basil ran to his dad's car, and they waved as I closed the door.

"I missed it, Maine. I missed it. I missed the first practice with our gear on."

"There will be a lot more peewees, peewee."

I ran him a nice warm bath to stew in.

"I don't understand. How did you get so sick so quickly?"

He shrugged.

"You were fine at breakfast."

He shrugged again and got into the bath. He didn't do his usual splash. No pep. No get-up-and-go. No zoom. Poor thing.

As I was putting his helmet and his shoulder and thigh pads back in his closet, I felt a tug on my shirt.

"I wonder what the team is up to right now," he said. He had the towel wrapped around him like a cape.

"Get back in the bathtub!" I screamed at him.

He turned and ran back into the bathroom, leaving more soggy child's-size-six footprints on the beige carpet. I went back to placing his things in the hamper.

I had only ten minutes more of peace.

He yelled at me from the head of the stairs. "I'm done with my bath."

"Good," I yelled back from the foot of the stairs.

"What do you want me to do now?"

"Get dressed in your pajamas. Do you need help?"

"No."

"Well, then, get into your jammies and get into bed. I'll be up there in a minute."

He coughed, then asked me, "What are you doing?"

"Never mind that. Just do what I ask."

"You tell me what you're doing, Maine."

"I am fixing you some soup, Tracy John."

He ran back into the bathroom.

I experienced a few more short moments of peace.

"What's holding up the soup?" he asked. At least he was in his pajamas. That was progress. "What kind of soup is it?" He was standing on his tippy-toes, trying to look into the pot.

"If you don't get back from the stove . . . ," I said.

He didn't move.

"Get away from the pot!" I raised my voice.

He jumped back and tried to show me his fang face, but instead he lapsed into a coughing fit.

"Why aren't you in bed resting?"

"I can't rest." He stomped his feet. "What kind of soup is it?" he asked.

I took a deep cleansing breath before I answered, "Chicken."

"Chicken noodle or cream of chicken?"

"Neither. Chicken with rice," I told him.

"I want tomato." He humphed and folded his arms. "When is Auntie going to be home?" he asked.

"Same time as usual."

His eyebrows shot up. "You ain't gonna call her so she can come home and take care of me?"

I patted his head. "You are in my care, sweet thang."

He ran away.

I thought I was safe; then I heard the theme song to *The Merv Griffin Show*. I went into the living room.

"Tracy John, you're not going to stay in here. Go up to your room."

He coughed. "I want to watch TV."

I stepped over to him. "I said go upstairs."

He sat back deeper in the sofa. "I don't want to."

I did my silent count to three and took a few more cleansing breaths. I smiled. "Oh, so now we're back on that again. I thought you were my friend."

"I am your friend. I'm your sick friend who wants to watch Merv."

I scooped him up. I held him in one arm while I turned off the set with my free hand. I went to the stairs and took each step with great stamina and determination till I got to the top; then I made a right turn and went straight to that middle room.

I set him on the bedspread, which had a brick pattern—brown and red bricks with white mortar oozing out.

I pulled his big blue blanket from the closet shelf. I lifted him up again, then slid him under the covers.

His little chin stuck out in shock. He hadn't known I was that strong. I was surprised myself; I had thought he'd be a lot heavier.

Out his window, a squirrel was on the maple tree, flicking its tail.

I held my pointer finger out to him and wagged it at him. "Now, stay where I put you."

At last, the soup was done. It was aromatic, and I was certain it would clear his sinuses. I put it on a tray and took it upstairs only to find him sound asleep. His wide little soft face seemed tranquil in dream.

I shook my head and smiled. I turned and headed for the door.

"Hey, where are you going with the soup?" he asked, peering through a squinting eye.

•••

After Ma got home, I overheard Tracy John's praise of me. "Maine took good care of me. She fed me soup. I feel"—he coughed—"one hundred percent better."

The next day, despite my TLC, Tracy John exhibited more cold symptoms, a redder nose, and a voice hoarser than Louis Armstrong's. Ma stayed home with him. In the afternoon, I came from school to find more complications.

"Guess what? Auntie got fired," Tracy John told me.

I searched his face for a trace of mockery. There was none. His eyes were wide with sincerity.

"Is it true?" I asked Ma.

She nodded.

"For missing one day?" I said.

"I was out that other day too, when we went up to see Miss Mullins."

"So that's only two days, Ma," I said.

"A lot of businesses don't understand how it is to raise a child."

"They hung up on her," Tracy John said while coughing and laughing.

"That's the way it goes sometimes." Ma shrugged, saying she would check on his soup.

Tracy John looked at me and said, "Soup, soup, soup! That's all I get! I'm sick of it! I hate being sick!"

I had learned to smile at his tirades. "Does it hurt to swallow?"

"No, my stomach hurts," he said.

I grinned and gave him a soft pat on his tummy. "Mucus travels down there."

That made his penny eyes open wide. He asked, "What's mucus?"

I leaned in close and put it in layman's terms. "Snot."

His full lips turned up at the corners. I'd known that would coax a smile out of him.

"You'll be all better for your peewee tomorrow."

"How do you know?"

"Because I am the maharaja."

"You're the what, now?" He folded his arms, sitting up in bed.

"The maharaja. All-seeing. All-knowing. All everything. Maha for short."

He tugged me. "Maha Maine, is Auntie going to get another job?"

Actually, my crystal ball was a little fuzzy on that one.

"Are we going to move to the poorhouse?"

"Tracy John, we are not going to move to the poorhouse."

"Is Uncle E going to turn himself in?"

"What do you know about Uncle E?"

"He's the reason we're broke, Maha Maine."

"We're not broke, Tracy John. We just temporarily don't have a lot of spare money."

"Is Santa Claus mad at us?" he asked.

"No, Santa Claus is very understanding."

"So he's still going to get me the LEGO set."

"That's not the meaning of Christmas, Tracy John. The meaning of Christmas is Jesus's birthday," I told him.

"Then Santa's not getting me the LEGO set?" he asked.

I grinned. "Daddy's working extra hours and Ma did save up some money from her job. We'll be all right."

After Ma brought the soup up to his room, I tried to feed it to him. He was resistant.

"I can't taste anything," he said. "And I missed the practice. I miss everything. Why couldn't I be sick last week when I was grounded?"

I pointed at him, putting two fingers to his mouth, and then made the peace sign. I spooned out a portion of the soup and put it right up to his lips.

"Open," I told him.

He did.

"Swallow."

He did.

"Good," I said, and winked at him.

He smiled at me.

Twelve

With things smoothed out between Tracy John and me, I felt definitely more focused—on Demetrius. My eyes were soft with affection for Demetrius McGee. I had him all to myself, right across from me at the kitchen table. He was wearing a pair of black slacks, creased and shiny, and a burgundy shirt. They were so in right then.

Yet he seemed distracted. He always seemed just a little not there even before Tracy John came into the middle of the room.

"Tracy John, what did I tell you about being a pest when I have company?"

"All I wanted to do was say hi," he said.

"Hello," I said, and spun him around, giving him a little slap on his bottom, much like a ranch hand did to a steer to get it to move.

As soon as I got rid of him and went back to my Demetrius, Leo came in.

"Will you go, Leo?"

"This is not off-limits," Leo argued. "I'm going to get a glass of milk, Maine."

"Get it quickly. And go."

"You need to calm down some," Leo told me.

"I'm sorry about all these interruptions," I said to Demetrius. "Now, where were we?"

"I want to do my paper on Martin Luther King."

"Great choice. There's so much on him. I even have a book by him. *Where Do We Go from Here: Chaos or Community?* I can lend—"

He pushed the U.S. history book away. "Look, why don't you just write it up?" he ventured, and then added, "I trust you."

I looked at him blankly.

"Just write the five pages." His voice was full and confident.

"You want me to write your term paper for you?" I asked in the hopes that I was guessing wrong.

He touched my hand, lightly, softly. And the rest of me tingled. He winked at me. "What's the difference? You've done plenty of work for me."

"This is not homework, Demetrius. This is graded."

"So?" he asked, again moving closer to me, his lips coming in for a landing on mine. I looked past him and saw Leo's and Tracy John's heads by the doorjamb.

"Excuse me, Demetrius." I stomped out to the living room.

"Don't do it," Leo pleaded.

Tracy John tapped me. "Maha Maine, you can't keep cheating for Demetrius."

Leo raised his fist in the air. "Right on."

I shut my eyes. "I don't need the peanut and the tap dance kid pressuring me."

"Demetrius's the one pressuring you," Leo said.

I couldn't muster a response. They were right. I knew that. It was just that I saw my whole future with Demetrius. We would go to the same college. I had my heart set on Howard University, the Ivy League school of black colleges. On our graduation night, he'd propose to me. Our engagement would last a little under a year. Then I'd be Mrs. Charmaine Upshaw-McGee. Our first house would be a town house in the city. Society Hill, perhaps.

"Why don't you do my homework too?" Tracy John asked.

"He's right. You might as well," Leo said. "How could you let yourself be used like this?"

"Yeah, how?" Tracy John asked.

"Enough, both of you." My heart was palpitating, my armpits were sweating, my pupils were probably dilating. Any moment, I was going to need blood pressure medication. *Relax. Relax, Maine.* "Tracy John and Leo, can I ask you a favor? Don't tell Ma or Daddy about this. Please. Pretty please." I folded my hands in prayer.

They both looked at me blankly, so I begged some more. I bowed and scraped.

"We won't say anything." Leo nudged Tracy John. "Will we, Tracy John?"

Tracy John was still considering it.

Leo pinched him; then he said okay.

Over the next week, I did a lot of soul-searching. The

homework that I'd done for Demetrius was bad enough, but writing someone's whole term paper and signing that person's name—wasn't that, like, really illegal?

Also, why hadn't Demetrius approached me with this earlier? Mr. Gowdy had given us this assignment way back in September. Back then, I had chosen to do mine on Fannie Lou Hamer, and my final draft had been done for weeks. All I had to do was type it. Over the next few days, I had to cram in all this research for Demetrius's paper.

I bit my lip as I typed. The first word was the hardest. *Martin.* There. *Luther. King,* I pecked, *was a man to be honored.*

Charmaine Mae Upshaw is a woman to be dishonored, I thought.

I typed quickly and accurately, making only two mistakes. Instead of whiting them out, I typed that page over again.

Fannie Lou Hamer was harder to type. Her mantra, "I'm sick and tired of being sick and tired," kept swimming through my mind.

Martin Luther King and Fannie Lou Hamer. Two people who stood for honesty and justice. And there I was straight-out lying.

Martin, Fannie, sorry.

In the end, I believed that writing two papers had been good for me. I had wanted a challenge.

When Ma peeked in on me, I casually flipped over the cover sheet that had Demetrius McGee's name on it.

She was full of chatter about how the eleven o'clock news was off and it was past my bedtime. But then she fixed me some chamomile tea and poured it into my favorite cup.

●●●

I finished typing and proofing both papers the following evening. I rang Demetrius to celebrate. I asked if he'd like to go to the movies or something. He told me he was too busy.

On the Monday due date, I saw Demetrius talking to Dinah on the school steps.

"Here." I shoved the paper at him and walked away from them.

"How else do you get someone like Demetrius to talk to you?" Dinah yelled after me.

Humiliation glowed within me like fire, but I walked on. It was done now.

Dinah ran up beside me with her swishy hair brushing against my forearm.

"He's still seeing me, Charmaine," she said.

I stopped walking. My fists were balled.

She backed up a few steps.

"Maine, it's not worth it," Millicent said, coming up to me and pulling me away. Cissy was with her.

When Dinah saw that, she just got meaner. "Buckwheat."

"If the fact that we're dark bothers you, I'd just like to tell you, we'd like to be light," Cissy screeched.

Millicent frowned. "That's telling her."

Dinah laughed and walked away. "You're all a bunch of losers."

"It takes one to know one," Millicent called after her.

Cissy turned to me. "It doesn't surprise me that Dinah is still going out with him. . . . I mean, Demetrius is cute. He's really cute."

"What is that supposed to mean?" I asked impatiently, perturbed. "I'm good enough for him. I'm better than her. He just doesn't know it."

What kind of fool did they think I was? I knew the score. If I could have taken back all my labor, I would have.

During fifth period, I had to listen to Mr. Gowdy sing the praises of Demetrius's (my) essay. He even asked him to present it in class the following day.

Demetrius winked at me.

● ● ●

I went home dejected. Totally crestfallen. Tracy John was making out a pretend Christmas list and a real one.

"Because Unc is mad at Santa Claus and there is an oil crisis," he explained.

"Tracy John, what do you know about the oil crisis?"

Tracy John looked at Leo, then said, "Jimmy Carter."

Leo gave him a thumbs-up.

"Do you want to add anything to my pretend Christmas list?" he asked.

"I know what Maine wants for Christmas— Demetrius," Leo said.

I growled at him. "Very funny. Put me down for a camera."

Tracy John busily scribbled my request; then he showed it to me. "Is that how you spell 'camera'?"

"Very good." I looked at his dream list, on which some thirty toys were enumerated, including that confounded LEGO set. "Your ma was a great photographer."

"What's that?" he asked, his brow furrowed with curiosity.

"Someone who takes pictures. And, boy, do I have photographs to prove it."

"Photographs?"

"Yes. Pictures."

"Pictures of what?"

"The three of us."

"Me and you?" His penny-colored eyes sparkled.

"And your mommy," I said.

"Where?"

"All over the place. Center City. Fairmount Park. Down Fifty-second Street. We even went to the Main Line once."

"Where?" he asked again.

"I'm telling you where."

"No. Where's your pictures?"

I waved him upstairs.

He flopped onto my bed and waited as I got my album out of the closet and opened it.

"Look at her copper eyes. Just like yours." I pointed to a candid close-up gathering.

He peered at it. "Ralph Pemberton said I had funny eyes."

"I believe I have heard enough from that ignorant Ralph Pemberton. Besides, he's only a first grader." And I quickly changed the subject to something I liked talking about—Auntie Karyn. "She was so pretty. Just like you."

"Boys ain't pretty," he said.

"You are. I guess that makes you a girl."

He made that fang face at me and pretended to claw at me.

I did a fake claw back at him. Even Steven.

"You have a lot of pictures." He was absorbed in the book.

"I told you I did."

I pointed at pictures of Tracy John with his tiny baby fists fighting with the air.

"You were a sweetheart," I said.

"Sweet thang," he said.

"Sweet thang," I said.

I pointed at one from when Auntie Karyn won the statewide "Why I Wanted to Be a Nurse" competition. That one touched a tender spot. Huge tears welled up in my eyes. I smiled sadly and leaned into my cousin.

Auntie Karyn had had a seven days on/five days off schedule. I remembered our day trips on those days off; we went to Center City. I remembered how the smells hit us: pungent foods, cars, and women's perfumes. We saw the showy buildings and baffling sculptures (a giant clothespin and blocked-out lettering of L-O, then V-E). Then, around Vine Street, we hit Chinatown, and there we heard another language (probably Mandarin). People prowled the streets on their way to somewhere. Once, we went to South Street. There I saw my first hippie.

"What's with that white man?" Tracy John asked, pointing in horror at a photo of this bearded, beaded man in Day-Glo.

"That's a hippie."

"Why is he dressed like a weirdo?"

"That was in then."

There was one of the three of us in front of a cramped little pizza shop on South Street, which was billed the best in the city.

"Who is that guy?" he asked, pointing at the man in the apron.

"The sauce guy."

"Did I get any pizza?" Tracy John asked.

"No. You were a little baby."

"Y'all still could have given me some," he insisted. "I like pizza."

I went into acting mode. "Oh, wait, let me remember that clearly. Auntie Karyn did give you some of her slice."

"And you gave me some of your slice, Maine."

"Of course." I nodded, playing along, pinching him.

Leo rushed in. "Maine, Maine, phone call—from Demetrius McGee," he said, holding his heart and making moon eyes.

"Tell him I'm busy," I said.

Leo looked around the room. "Doing what?"

"Maine was showing me pictures," Tracy John said.

Intrigued, Leo advanced. "Pictures?"

All three of us sat on my twin bed, flipping slowly through the pages.

Thirteen

Like cheese in a mousetrap, Demetrius was waiting by my locker. But, for once, I didn't bite. "Where were you when I called?" he asked.

"Well, hello, Demetrius," I said. "How are you?"

"I wanted to tell you something last night."

"So tell me now." I squared off.

"Why didn't you call me back?" he asked.

I looked him dead in the eye. "I guess because I didn't feel like it."

"Charmaine, I need you to make me up some notes."

"Notes?"

His wording was simple and transparent. "Yes, notes. For my U.S. history speech."

"Demetrius, you can't even make your own speech from the essay I wrote for you?"

"I didn't have time to read that."

"Don't do it, Maine," Millicent said, coming up behind me.

"Why don't you shut your fat mouth?" Demetrius yelled at Millicent.

"Hey, hey," I said, but I was unable to get anything more out. He was insulting my best friend, yet all I was able to muster was this mumbling, lame protest.

The bell rang for first period.

"Put it on three-by-five cards. Real big so I can read it," he told me, as if issuing a military order.

As Millicent and I hurried down the hall, she asked me, "That's what Dinah was squawking about? You've been doing his homework for him? Why?"

"I didn't do all his homework."

"However much you did, why did you do it?"

"What do you think?" I said as I reached French class.

"That's not ethical," Millicent said.

"No kidding," I said.

At lunch, I had to hear more of this. Millicent had told Cissy, and they both lambasted me for being so wrong.

"I don't know what's wrong with you people; you act like you don't know how much I like him. I would do anything for Demetrius. If he asked me to swallow nails, I would. Who are y'all going out with?"

Cissy craned her neck. "The same person you are, Maine—nobody."

I craned my neck right back at her. "Cissy, Demetrius will be my boyfriend; it's just a matter of time."

"Months, years, decades . . . ," Millicent said.

"I have a relationship with Demetrius," I insisted, stomping my foot.

"You have a courier service with Demetrius," Millicent said.

I stood up. I took my bag lunch—meat loaf from the night before on wheat bread—and my juice carton and tossed it all out. I walked the corridor without a hall pass. I had a purposeful walk. I knew I wouldn't get in trouble. I was an angel—even better than an angel. I was "the smart girl."

It was 12:10. I still had time to write something for Demetrius.

I sat on the steps in the east wing. I'd never known how much dirt was there, especially in the corners. Cobwebs and filth. No matter, though, I wasn't wearing anything all that nice. Just an old blue knit dress that had a few snags. I bet for Christmas I was going to get another knit dress.

I hoped I wouldn't get any taller. I was already a freak of nature, towering over most boys in my grade. I was teacher sized.

I also hoped I would start to develop soon, so that Demetrius could want to be with me for reasons other than my brain.

I checked my watch: two minutes to Mr. Gowdy's class.

I wasn't going to write anything.

My stomach and scalp tingled.

Next thing I knew, the bell rang.

Mr. Gowdy always just started class, never offering any

small talk or comments about the weather. He got straight to business. We took our seats, and he introduced Demetrius as the presenter that day.

Demetrius looked at me. I looked steadily back at him, not giving him one inch. A telltale tic in his jaw jumped; then he regained his composure. Demetrius wore his charismatic smile all the way up to the podium.

"What can you tell us about Martin Luther King?" Mr. Gowdy asked Demetrius in his heavy Brooklynese.

Demetrius cleared his throat. "Martin Luther King . . . ," he said. Nothing followed.

"Demetrius, please, please run over the highlights."

Demetrius gulped. "The highlights?"

"Yes, Demetrius."

"Martin Luther King?"

"Yes." Mr. Gowdy gestured wildly for him to continue.

Demetrius gripped the podium. "Martin Luther King . . . Martin Luther King."

Silence.

Then Demetrius said, "Martin Luther King was a man."

A few people snickered.

"Yes. . . . Tell us about the Montgomery bus boycott."

Demetrius looked perplexed. "The what?"

Mr. Gowdy's eyebrows went together. He crossed his legs. "You put it in your paper."

"I did? I mean, I did, but I really can't . . . You know what I mean?"

Mr. Gowdy shook his head. "No, I don't. . . . Why don't you tell us about his letter from the Birmingham jail."

"Martin Luther King was a jailbird?"

"He was jailed over thirty times, Demetrius."

"What was he, a shoplifter?"

I turned so that he couldn't see me snicker.

"Are you asking me? This is your presentation. Do you remember anything from your research?"

Demetrius cleared his throat again and said, "Lee Harvey Oswald shot Martin Luther King."

"You mean James Earl Ray," Mr. Gowdy corrected.

"Well, it was somebody with three names," Demetrius snapped.

He looked up and smiled again. "Martin Luther King. Martin Luther King was a man."

Mr. Gowdy smiled knowingly. "I think you've said enough."

I looked back at Millicent, who was laughing so hard that tears were coming out of her eyes. She was hitting the desk. She raised her hand to be excused.

I raised my hand too.

Millicent and I made it into the lavatory and totally lost it. We fell into each other, laughing.

"He said Martin Luther King was a shoplifter," Millicent howled, drying her eyes on paper towels. "He is so pathetic."

We were still yukking it up in chemistry class. I noticed that Demetrius wasn't there, and that somehow added to the hilarity. I figured he was somewhere kicking his rear end about the whole thing.

After school, though, he caught me by my locker.

"Who do you think you are?" he asked.

"A person who's not feeding you answers," I said, stepping up to him.

"You made me look like a fool up there, Charmaine."

"I've been covering for you, prolonging the inevitable, Demetrius. But there's one thing you must know: every road eventually turns. You can't use people forever."

"You let me use you. You wanted me to."

"And now I don't want you to."

"You know something? You are a bitch." He stepped back and smiled as if he'd gained his little victory.

I rolled my eyes. Big deal, he'd used a cuss word. Like I was supposed to be impressed.

My admonishing finger waved back and forth at him. I said, "I may be a bitch, Demetrius. But at least I know history."

● ● ●

At dinner, I told my family about Demetrius's fiasco. I neglected to mention that I'd written the original paper.

"That boy couldn't say anything else?" Daddy shook his head in disgust while passing the rolls counterclockwise. "What a jive turkey."

Leo took a roll. "He must have looked like a real dummy."

"Martin Luther King wanted peace," Tracy John said, and held up four fingers. "And he has this many kids."

"That is a damn shame. Even little Tracy John knows more than he does," Daddy said.

"He could have talked about the famous speech at the Lincoln Memorial," Leo said.

"He also got that big, big prize," Ma said, sipping ice water before taking a bite of her spinach, chicken, and rice casserole.

"The Nobel Peace Prize," Leo said.

" 'I am cognizant of the interrelatedness of all communities and states. I cannot sit idly by in Atlanta and not be concerned about what happens in Birmingham. Injustice anywhere is a threat to justice everywhere. We are caught in an inescapable network of mutuality, tied in a single garment of destiny. Whatever affects one directly, affects all indirectly,' " Daddy said, quoting Martin Luther King.

A rainfall of clapping followed.

Tracy John said, "Right on, Unc!"

Daddy was an excellent orator. As opposed to Demetrius in his white shirt and pin-striped tie, Daddy, in his T-shirt and dungarees, could rattle off a critical response just speaking loosely. The funny thing was that Daddy always disparaged his mere ninth-grade education, but I believed that he was the smartest person in the world.

Fourteen

The following day, I took Tracy John to the library. Together, we read about the solar system and dinosaurs; then
we read Aesop's fable about the fox and the stork. The fox
invited the stork over for dinner and served soup in a shal-
low dish, though physically the stork was incapable of
eating soup. The stork reciprocated by inviting the fox
over for a supper, which he served in a tall narrow glass.

Moral of the story: one bad turn deserves another.

"You are the stork, cuz you have a long neck," Tracy
John said to me.

Nothing could spoil my shimmering mood, certainly
not being told that I had a scrawny throat. But then I ran
into a couple who threatened my ease. Until then, I had
thought the library was a G-rated place. There they were
by the section that hardly anyone used, the section dedicated to seniors, called Fifty-Plus. Dinah, with her fair
skin and long glamorous locks, grabbed Demetrius's face

and kissed it. She pressed against him, massaging his bottom.

Something tightened inside me. Tracy John tugged on my sleeve, asking, "Why is he with her?"

"I don't know, Tracy John. Hush, this is a library."

"What is he doing with her?" He took it down to a medium volume.

I threw him a peace sign.

He gave me a quizzical look.

"Peace, Tracy John." Then I covered my lips.

He pinched me. "She did like this."

"Ouch!" I exclaimed, and swatted his hands away. I decided that this was a good time to leave, so we gathered up our books and went to the counter.

From the back room, a short redheaded lady came out. She spoke with a clogged voice. "Well, well, what a cute little boy."

"This is Tracy John."

"When do I get my own card?" he asked.

"You don't need your own card. You can use mine," I told him.

"He's adorable!" the librarian exclaimed. "Let me get him something." That happened quite a bit when I was with Tracy John. People would give him a sticker or a lollipop. If they didn't have a trinket handy, they would run into the back and look around for something. The librarian came back smiling big and handed him a bookmark with a worm on it.

"Say thank you to Mrs. Latimer, Tracy John."

Tracy John said, "Thank you."

The librarian asked, "Say, would you two mind being in a picture?"

She brought a camera from the back room, explaining that this would make lovely publicity to show to the board members. We went back to the children's section. I patted Tracy John's head to make sure his 'fro was even. I straightened his shirt and told him to smile.

"She didn't say cheese," he said.

"It's so rare that I see a big sister and a little brother get along so well," Mrs. Latimer said.

At that, Tracy John smiled.

The librarian took an extra shot for us to keep. I showed it to Daddy when he came home. "Now, who are these two celebrities?" he asked.

"Me and Maine," Tracy John said, beaming.

"You two make a lovely couple." He nodded admiringly. "Don't they, Miss Sweet Thang?"

"My, my, my," Ma said, and took a break from battering the okra. She dried her hand on her apron. "You two look so darling."

I placed the picture on the fridge under plastic butterfly magnets.

Fifteen

The following Sunday, as I was leaving church, the reverend pulled me to the side, saying, "I can't think of a more fitting young lady to deliver the Kwanzaa address. You have such poise and grace. Such beauty."

"Beauty?" I blushed vividly.

I smiled. That kind of thing *never* happened to me. I was picked out of the crowd for my brains but never my looks.

Now there was only one small thing I had to do. I had to find out exactly what Kwanzaa was. I knew that it was something like a black Christmas. Oddly enough, though, this holiday wasn't religious. The school library had nothing on it, but I knew that Dardon Public wouldn't let me down.

I took Tracy John and pored over books till suppertime; then we lugged as many as we could home. The following day, he had peewee practice, but the day after that, Tracy John was front and center asking, "Are we going to read about Kwanzaa?"

"Maybe later. Right now we have to visit Cissy and Millicent."

"We? Me too?"

"That's what I said. Get your coat."

He wasn't budging. "They're boring."

I shook my head. "Tracy John, not that again. Don't be that way. Both Cissy and Millicent want you to come over because they got you a present."

"A present for me?" he asked. He wore a look of total confusion.

"Of course. You're their friend."

"I am?"

"You're gonna like this present."

"Tell me what it is?"

I resisted his urgings and insisted that he go to pick it up.

"They say nice things about you."

"They do?"

"All the time. You know that. And I'll tell you something else; every time we have a fight, they always take your side."

He stood up. "I'll get my coat."

Cissy's place smelled like her baby niece's throw-up, but her niece, sisters, and mother were gone for the afternoon, leaving us with this combination living room, rec room, den, kitchen, and baby's room to ourselves. Cissy had the table kicked back and standing on its end.

"What day does the maid come in?" Tracy John asked me.

I threw him the peace sign.

"Hi, T.J.," Cissy greeted him.

He looked behind him. "Who's T.J.?"

Cissy pointed at him. "That's you. Sometimes it takes too long to say your whole name."

"I ain't gonna be no letters. I'm gonna be a name. Two names. Tracy and John."

"You are so cute." Cissy hugged him.

"My turn," Millicent said, and got in her squeeze.

She asked me, "Should we give him the present now, or should we make him wait?"

"You should give it to me now," he answered.

Millicent ran into the hall and came back with a big box. Tracy John took it, held it to his ear and shook it, pulled at the ribbon, and took off the glossy wrapping paper, which featured snowmen. He opened the box and jumped for joy.

"This is the best present ever!" he said. I'd known he'd love it. It was a Dallas Cowboys jersey with the last name Upshaw stenciled on the back. That, of course, would totally ruin him for what I had gotten him: Spider-Man jammies that were red and blue with black webbing over the top.

We helped him put the jersey on over his turtleneck. During another round of hugs, he told them, "I'm sorry I said y'all were boring."

Silence.

"What?" Millicent and Cissy asked in unison.

"What?" Tracy John asked, turning to me, feigning surprise.

God, he was good. He could turn on the innocence on

a dime. "What?" I asked him back; then I covered for him. "What difference did it make?"

• • •

On Tuesday night, Tracy John came to the door of my room, carrying his pillow and his favorite blanket.

"I asked Leo if I could swap for tonight."

"Why?" I asked him.

He answered me in one word: "Snow."

Tracy John peered out my window. Snow was falling lightly outside. "You have the best view in the house. So can I stay?"

"Of course."

"Solid," he said. "Do you think we'll get tomorrow off?"

"It'll have to pick up," I said.

"I like snow, but I don't like hail," he said.

"What do you have against hail, Tracy John?"

"Hail is noisy and scary."

"Scary? You're scared of hail?"

"Kinda. Does that make me a baby?"

"Of course."

"It does?"

"You are a baby. You're the baby of the family. You don't have to be brave," I told him. "That's what you have us for, your family." I kissed him between his eyeballs.

• • •

131

Well into that night, I felt it in my underpants and saw sticky redness down my upper thighs. *Yes!* I thought. I got up, stripped the bed, and went into the bathroom to clean myself. I put on fresh undies and a nightgown. Then I went to the closet and got out a new pair of sheets.

Tracy John sat bolt upright, asking incredulously, "Did you wet the bed?"

I shook my head and told him to go back to sleep.

"What happened, then?" he asked.

I thought of a way to delicately put it. "I went through a change."

He lost interest. He lay back down, rolled over, and said, "The change of the sheets."

The next day, the sky was clear. The snow hadn't stuck, and I went to junior high Kotex-strapped and head up. I was proud. I told Cissy and Millicent before class, and they squealed and jumped up and down and welcomed me to the club.

At supper, Tracy John said, "Auntie told me all about your lady time."

"My what?" I exclaimed, embarrassed.

"No need to make things a mystery," Daddy said. "We all got to know about everybody's everything."

"Does everybody know?" I asked.

Leo came into the room, nodding and saying, "Yes."

• • •

My period lasted a whole five days, which took me right up to Horace's graduation from basic, and what a day that was.

Fort Dix was a forty-five-minute station wagon drive from Philadelphia. Tracy John sat between Leo and me, and we were all jazzed with anticipation as we cruised down the rustic Route 38. We were actually going to see an army base. We rounded the gate and saw a group sitting on duffel bags; then we drove past the confidence course and saw soldiers scaling walls. We saw the Main Post Exchange, which looked pretty much like Kmart.

We found the auditorium, where several flags were displayed, Old Glory and one with the battalion insignia of a fierce fire-breathing lion among them. Map reading, bivouac, range fire, first aid, D and C, and BRM all boiled down to this.

In the bleacher seats, some people were in dress greens, and some were in civvies. People waved small American flags.

The ceremony began with a lecture about the need for soldiers even in peacetime.

I hardly recognized Horace; he blended in so well.

The soldiers looked like green ants. I should have brought my dollar-store binoculars.

Then came the reading of the graduates' names. The officer instructed us to hold our applause until all names were read. Sensing the inevitable, I looked over at Leo and Tracy John. The drill floor was silent, and then the familiar name was called. "Horace Peyton Upshaw."

Leo and Tracy John exploded with clapping and hooting. The boys threw homemade confetti in the air. Everyone turned and looked at us.

After the rest of the names were read, they announced the most distinguished soldier of the term. To my surprise, my brother's name was called again. Horace strutted up to the podium with his skinny, slack-hipped physique. He shook hands with his commanding officer. Cameras snapped away. I wondered if he'd be in the newspaper the next day.

Leo and Tracy John made more noise. "Go 'head, Horace!" they yelled.

After the ceremony, we posed for Polaroids. High-rankers still clamored about Horace, so they got in most of the shots. We worked all combinations. There was one with me and Horace and a general.

"Wow, soldier of the cycle!" Leo exclaimed.

"My boy is a born leader," Daddy said.

Ma cried, as usual.

Next, we went to the mess hall. That was a different experience from what Horace had described. He'd said he had five minutes to eat meals that looked like slop. Yet a gorgeous spread was out for the benefit of these grunts' loved ones. There were fried shrimp, porterhouse steaks cooked to order, baked potatoes, and garlic bread. We ate leisurely.

"I don't know what you complained about, Horace. This is good food," Leo said.

"We call it chow," Horace said.

"This is good chow," Tracy John said.

I felt Horace's head, ~which was smooth and darn near bald.

"Your buddy Claude almost has his 'fro back," I said.

"He really made a boomerang back to Dardon," Leo said.

Daddy nodded. "The army's not for everyone."

• • •

On his holiday leave, Horace came home and settled back into his same routine. Horace, Leo, and Tracy John shoveled the walk. Flakes caught in Leo's and Tracy John's 'fros but rolled off Horace's Mr. Clean do. As always, they did more playing than clearing a path in the snow. I stuck to my usual inside work, helping Ma with dinner, but when I ventured outside to tell them to get ready for supper, I heard someone say "Get her."

I turned just in time to get one in the face.

I scooped up a good ball. "Which one of you did it?"

I couldn't figure out which, so I threw one at each of them. I missed all three.

• • •

After a few more days of snow-clogged trees, I was sick of the great outdoors. While I was flipping through *Seventeen* magazine, Horace said to me, "I need another hand. I'm clearing things away."

I took an up-and-down look at him. His dashiki and wide-legged pants went better with his afro. Civilian clothes and military haircut: it just didn't work.

"Hire the Russian army," I told him. "They aren't busy."

"Come on." He pulled me to my feet.

"Why don't you ask Leo?" I said.

"I'm asking you."

He marched me up to the attic. I found his things boxed and tagged. The sliding closet was cleared. His idea was to put each box in, stacking one on top of the other. I took a box, and we began the two-person assembly line.

"I don't know why you're complaining," he told me. "I'm clearing things out for you."

I stopped cold. My own room? My privacy? That was what I had longed for, wasn't it? I had nearly forgotten. I certainly hadn't thought it would be like this, way up here away from the rest of the family.

Horace swiveled his head toward me. "You're not jumping for joy. I thought this was what you wanted. What changed?"

Very good question. I thought back to two weeks before, when Ma had taken Tracy John and me to the supermarket. Around aisle ten, Ma met up with a friend of hers and was distracted in conversation. Tracy John rode on the side of the shopping cart to the next aisle. I followed him. Though the cart was filled to the brim, I wasn't concerned. This was what he always did. Then I saw it turning over, and I rushed to the other side of it to balance it.

As if I needed any other clue that I could stand to bulk up on Dunkin' Donuts, or at least lunch on a whole sandwich rather than a half of one, I couldn't hold the line. The momentum was too great, and I found myself traveling with Tracy John and the cart.

"Help us!" I screamed as our descent accelerated. Tracy John and I faced imminent crushing.

Just then, a bald, tall, brown-skinned man who sort of resembled James Earl Jones did a double take, then sprang into action. He charged over from the end of the aisle, by the Tater Tots, and leveraged the cart back to its rightful stand.

Tracy John and I both tumbled free. I thought my skirt came up briefly, but I didn't care. I was so happy to be alive. "Thanks, mister," I said.

The man offered me a hand up and rubbed Tracy John on the head.

"Yeah, thanks, mister," Tracy John said.

The man just tipped his head and walked away.

I turned to Tracy John. "We could have been killed! Crushed by falling food!"

He swallowed, shaken by the experience. "I'm sorry."

"Don't you ever, ever, ever do that again!"

"I won't." He tugged at my sleeve; those penny-colored eyes of his were stretched wide. "Maha Maine? Are you going to tell Auntie?"

"No."

"You ain't gonna tell?"

"I'm not going to tell on you, Tracy John," I promised. I realized something from that experience. That man, whom I didn't know and probably would never see again, didn't have to get involved. I loved the way he did it. No fanfare. He just smiled and walked back to do the rest of his shopping.

Horace shoved me. "Earth to Charmaine. Come in, Charmaine. What's come over you? What changed?"

"I did."

He cast me a slanted glance of curiosity, then nodded knowingly. "I knew you'd hold things together. Just like Hoss on the Ponderosa."

I put my hands on my imagination. "For the last time, you're Hoss. I'm Audra."

• • •

Later that day, I went to pick up Tracy John from Basil's place. Demetrius came to the door. "Daisy took them to the park." My heart didn't leap as our eyes met. He was still handsome close up, but he just didn't do it for me anymore.

"Oh." I turned to walk down the steps. "I'll come back in a little while, then."

"Charmaine," he called to me.

I turned toward him.

"Mr. Gowdy failed me in that class. I'll have to attend summer school. It was hardly worth it."

I shrugged and said, "Are you telling me?"

"Mr. Gowdy really laid into me."

"I'm sorry I missed that." I walked to the front gate.

"Maine, I could have said your name. I could have said it was all your fault."

"My fault? My fault?" I asked him. "I can't believe I ever thought you were something special."

I saw Daisy coming up the driveway, followed by Basil and Tracy John. When Tracy John saw me, he ran right into my arms. "Maha!" he said.

"He calls you Mama?" Demetrius asked me.

"No," Tracy John said. "I call her Maha. It's short for Maharaja. All-seeing and all-knowing."

Demetrius looked at him like he was crazy; then he looked at me like I was crazy. Then he shook his head at both of us and turned to go back into the house.

"Demetrius," Tracy John called to him before he closed the door.

"What?" Demetrius asked.

"You jive turkey," Tracy John said; then we stuck our tongues out at him and ran.

Sixteen

Slavery lasted several hundred years; for many, slavery of the mind was still going on. On December 22, I decided to free myself, to go totally natural. I decided to wear a bush. This saved a half hour of my life that first week alone. Also, I didn't have to worry about getting it wet. Bye-bye, hot comb. Good riddance, hair grease.

I borrowed a dashiki from Horace and put on some work jeans and tennis sneakers.

"You look like a different person," Leo said.

"You look like a soul sister," Tracy John said.

"That looks very attractive," Daddy said. "That style is you."

Later at school, most of my teachers gave me the eye, but no one commented except for Mr. Gowdy. "We have a new person in class. Would you care to introduce yourself?" he asked, smiling.

The next day, I did something new with my Afro. I

tied a scarf around it. Not a rag—a scarf. It was mesh, which accentuated my long neck.

"You stopped straightening your hair! Are you insane?" Dinah asked.

I was so steeled, so resolute, that Dinah's obligatory rude comment didn't even faze me.

"Dinah, you wouldn't understand."

"You look like a real African," she said, biting off the words of this supposed insult.

I smiled and said, "Thank you."

She looked at me like I was possessed. Before she escaped down the hall, I said to her, "Dinah, s-o-l-i-d-a-r-i-t-y. Not only can I spell it, but I know what it means."

By the time chemistry rolled around, I was looking forward to the time off from her and only seeing the people from school who I wanted to see, which meant Millicent and Cissy. Or so I thought. At my locker, I sorted through the books I needed to take for the holidays.

"What are you doing for break?" asked Spiderman.

I turned to him, noting his tiny cramped shoulders and broad smiling face.

I smiled too and said, "Stuff with church. Stuff with my family. What about you, Spiderman?"

"I'm going to Virginia to see my grandparents, but I won't be gone for the whole vacation. Maybe we could go out for a soda or something."

"I don't know; I'll probably be busy."

"Oh," he said, dejected. He tapped my locker and turned to leave. "Maybe some other time, then."

I stopped him. "Wait, maybe you'd like to attend this thing at my church. I'm emceeing the first part of it."

"You are?" he asked, his eyes sparkling again.

"Yep. It's an all-day thing for Kwanzaa. Drop in whenever you want."

•••

Christmas came and went. Tracy John didn't get his LEGO set; he got the cheaper Lincoln Logs. That seemed to make him just as happy.

Like on every holiday, Gammy came over. She was dressed very nicely in an above-the-knees poly-rayon dress with mitered stripes. I told her about the program I was planning at church, listing blacks' accomplishments.

"That'll be a short program," Gammy told me.

"Ma," Daddy said.

"All we did was invent peanut butter and sing 'We Shall Overcome,' " Gammy said.

"Ma, please."

"What's that month when we run down all our accomplishments?" Gammy said.

"February, Ma."

"Pretty soon we're going to have these whites thinking that they didn't do anything. They might get an inferiority complex."

"I don't think that will happen, Gammy," Horace told her.

"Who's that black man who did the first open-heart surgery?" Ma asked.

"Daniel Hale Williams," Daddy said.

"He's called the father of biology," I said.

"He's kind of late to be the father of biology. He was around at the beginning of the century?"

"Maybe he's the father of modern biology, Ma," Daddy said.

Gammy just humphed. "He must be the first black to pass biology in high school."

Horace fell out at that.

For all Gammy's wisecracks, she told me she would make a point to attend church with us that Sunday instead of the church in the city she usually attended with her sister. She told me she wouldn't miss my emceeing for the world.

•••

Later, I used Horace, Leo, and Tracy John as my audience while I practiced my speech.

"Kee-nar-ra. Kinara," I said. "This is a candleholder that holds seven candles, and they represent our family background and where we are from. Now, repeat after me, all of you. Mishumaa saba. Mee-shoo-ma sa ba."

"What kind of word is that?" Tracy John got flip.

I shot him a look, and he put his two fingers over his closed lips and made a peace sign with the other hand.

"And the red is for blood." I handed him the candle.

Tracy John recoiled. "Yuck."

"The blood, the pain that we have suffered all these years. The people suffered so that they can prosper.

"The green candles mean land." I handed them to Leo. "And there're three of them, and the black means people." I handed the black candle to Horace.

Horace asked, "Only one brother?"

•••

I had a lot of work to do with this Kwanzaa business. Like any great leader, I knew that my success hinged upon my distribution of this responsibility. I decided to have a little activity for people Tracy John's age. I was going to have them report on famous black scientists and doctors. I had the boys and girls of the congregation draw for names. Tracy John drew Meredith Gourdine.

Daddy asked what she had done.

"Meredith is a he, Daddy," I softly corrected.

Daddy smiled. "He should call himself Meredith John."

I worked on Tracy John's posture, his elocution, his eye contact, and his hand gestures. Not that it was a contest, but I was certain he was going to be the best presenter.

Late that Saturday night, I felt a tug at my shoulder.

"I can't do that Meredith Gourdine speech. I'm too scared," Tracy John said to me.

"Scared? You?" I rubbed my eyes.

"I don't want to get up there in front of all those people."

I smiled. He was wearing the Spider-Man jammies I had bought him. For anything else, he had a mouth. He inserted himself into the spotlight time and time again.

What was so different about getting up in front of our congregation?

"Tracy John, you're someone who's kind of shy but kind of not," I said, and sat up. "This is the most important thing you will do all year."

He frowned. "The year is almost over."

"Exactly. You must echo the sentiments of our ancestors."

"What's an ancestor?"

"The people of the past. The people we love who are gone. Do it for Sojourner Truth, Denmark Vesey, and Medgar Evers."

"I don't know any of those people."

"They know you. They sacrificed for you. They gave their lives for you, Tracy John. That's why this presentation is so important."

"Why don't y'all go in the other room if you're going to carry on a full conversation," Leo griped from his bed.

I got out of bed and took Tracy John by the hand. I led him back to his room and said in a low voice, "Tracy John, you must stand tall and proud like our ancestors and tell—tell not only Friendship AME church but the world."

"But what if I can't remember everything? What if I get up there and make a fool out of myself like Demetrius?"

"Demetrius is a fake. He didn't study. He didn't practice. He thinks that just because people like him, he's too good to work. You are nothing like him. You're very hardworking and I know tomorrow you are going to be perfect."

A few hours later, on that beautiful Sunday morning, I saw Daddy shaved, suited, and with shoes shined. He winked at us. Tracy John asked him, "Unc, you're coming to church?"

"I wouldn't miss you and Maine for the world. Besides, I'm down with Christ," he told us. He joined his brown hand with Ma's white-gloved one and they walked arm in arm.

Reverend Clee was as superb as he had been the week prior.

"If you are right, God will fight your battles," cried out the reverend.

"Preach, preacher," affirmed Ma's friend, Mrs. Langley.

"We are gonna get real black up in here," Reverend Clee said to us.

Daddy held up his hand. "Don't hurt nobody, Rev."

"We are dark-skinned people."

"Take your time," Mrs. Langley said.

"We are broad-nosed people."

"Tell it," Mr. Harvey said.

"We are large-lipped people."

"All right now," Daddy said.

"Now, this much-maligned facial configuration is the source of envy the world around. Thusly, you will never hear me say 'Make me whiter than snow' from this pulpit. I've heard that some of us are even ashamed of being black. Be who we are, and we are going to show the whole wide world that we are in love."

Next the choir sang. Our rev even sang a little, and his voice was surprisingly soft, like custard.

My turn came next. I did the emcee bit and turned it over to the congregation's children. One by one, each kid mumbled a rushed, nonenunciated garble of words relating to our history. The next-to-last girl to speak dropped the microphone.

I helped reorganize things and went into my final introduction.

Tracy John took the podium. He looked very classy for a child. Very distinguished, like royalty. (I'm not talking like King Louis or Henry the Eighth. I'm talking Shaka Zulu or Cinque.) To see him in his gray suit and maroon tie was nothing compared to hearing his elegant delivery.

"Meredith Gourdine," he said in a voice that boomed, "is a physicist who was born in 1929. He is known for his pioneering work in electrogasdynamics, or as it's called in scientific circles, EGD."

The congregation clapped.

"That's our boy," Daddy yelled out.

Horace and Leo cheered.

Ma was, of course, blubbering away.

As proud as they were of Tracy John, that pride multiplied by a million was my sentiment.

Mrs. Clee was down from Minneapolis; she offered her handshake, warm and firm, and she kissed us. She was wearing a majestic purple robe, like Jesus. There was a gap between her front teeth. Her hair was unprocessed, like mine. The reverend held his wife as if she was a treasure made from gold.

In the afternoon of this all-day affair, we girls wore the same dress. The males stripped down, taking off their suit coats.

Spiderman was there. He was wearing clothes that

matched for a change. He looked almost handsome. He said hello to me, then turned to Tracy John.

"Hey, you really know your stuff, little man."

"I have a great coach," Tracy John told him as I hugged his shoulders.

Many other people came up to congratulate Tracy John on his dramatic-speaking ability. They swept him away, so it was just Spiderman before me.

"Thanks for coming, Spiderman," I said.

"You can call me Raymond," he said, and gave me a penetrating look. Then he took my hand.

"Thank you, Raymond," I said, blushing a little from the attention.

In the church's rec room, the food committee had gone beyond sheet cake and punch. They were almost in funeral mode with this elaborate spread. Chicken was well represented. Fried, broiled, baked . . . Greens. Potato, macaroni, and three-bean salads. The committee had also cut cheese sandwiches into little angels.

After brunch, Reverend Clee delivered libation: words of hope and prosperity. "By celebrating this day, I acknowledge that those who came before me have run their races and that it's time for me to run mine."

He raised a cup and passed it to Tracy John, who just happened to be standing right next to him. Tracy John downed the whole cup.

Everyone looked at him and laughed.

"Where are we gonna get more libation?" Tracy John asked.

I took his hand and the cup. "From the kitchen sink, where else?"

We went to the back room. He climbed up on the counter and sat as I let the water run to cold.

Tracy John tugged on my dress. "Is Spiderman your boyfriend now?"

I just patted his head and remained silent. He didn't have to know everything. I filled up the cup.

"Is my mommy an ancestor like Martin Luther King?" he asked me. His penny-colored eyes shone bright and clear. "You said people who died are ancestors."

I turned to him. Ma, Daddy, Leo, Horace, Millicent, and Cissy had been right all along: the relationship between Tracy John and me had been a friendship delayed. I started tearing up, thinking of all that I would have missed if I had kept on the same blind path I had been on. Much as I had seen Auntie Karyn, I now saw her only son as a neon rainbow. Bright. Strong. Beautiful. He was a part of her. How could I ever have had anything but love for him?

"Are you all right?" he asked.

"Yes. I'm just so happy. I know that your mommy can see you. Tracy John, she's so proud of you."

His thumb brushed away the streaks of tears from my face. It was just like that saying: a person is never dead until the memory of that person is forgotten. I pulled him down from the counter, and then we went back to the celebration.

About the Author

A Philadelphia native and a Virgo, Allison Whittenberg studied dance for years before switching her focus to writing. She has an MA in English from the University of Wisconsin and enjoys traveling to places such as the Caribbean and Russia. *Sweet Thang* is her first novel.